GRACE OF THE MONARCHS

& Her Miraculous Journey

by
G.H. BABAGILO

This book is dedicated to
my family and friends
and all the caterpillars out there
who want to fly

Acknowledgments

Grace of the Monarchs was partially inspired by two female butterflies, Daphna and Jenny B the Tiger, whose transformations I had the privilege of watching first hand. Special thanks to my wonderful editor Elaine Partnow.

Prologue

Dear Traveler,

You are about to embark on a miraculous journey. You need no baggage, no heavy backpack, not even a walking stick. On this journey you will travel light.

Right now, in the depths of your soul, lies a caterpillar. Be still. Quiet your mind. Can you feel it stirring within you? This lowly creature will help you smash the shackles of doubts and fears that limit you. You will crawl like a bug no more! Rather, fly into the light!

But before you do, the caterpillar within you must die.

Do not fear, do not weep. The death of your caterpillar is not the end, but the joyous awakening of the real you.

Wake up, butterfly! Wake up! Burst free of your limited shell and emerge with your butterfly wings. The world around you is filled with color and light. Flap your golden wings. Fly— and you shall see for yourself!

CHAPTER 1

The clock at Grace's office showed 1:00 p.m. She packed her notebook, files, and calendar into her black leather bag and rushed out through the corridor.

"Happy birthday, Grace," her peers called as she passed their gray cubicles. She forced some fake smiles and nodded, unable to utter a word through her constricted throat.

The long hallway finally ended. When Grace stepped out of the glass door, her wet hazel eyes threatened to overflow with tears. "Hold on..." she mumbled as she entered the elevator. Luckily, no one was inside. She pressed the P button. Now she had more than thirty floors to collect herself.

As the elevator began to descend, Grace stared at the mirror. Under her exhausted eyes were puffy bags and black circles no makeup could hide, signs of long sleepless nights full of tears. The bright smile that could once light a dim room remained hidden behind tight lips. The smooth amber hair that fell on her slender back appeared as dull as her face.

Being a lawyer in a top-notch firm, she found herself often in black and gray business suits. Her least favorite colors, they seemed fitting now.

"Gong!" The elevator doors opened and she hurried on her high heels to her silver Mercedes.

Toronto downtown streets were hectic and busy as a beehive on a spring day. Her sweaty palms gripped the wheel as though she was driving for the first time. Leaving for her office before sunrise and returning home late at night, Grace had forgotten what heavy traffic felt like. She couldn't remember the last time she had left her workplace midday.

"Too early to go to my empty home," she muttered.

She stopped by a park. Golden and red maple leaves covered the grass as she strolled along a crusty path. The afternoon sun penetrated the vibrant foliage and painted the ground in ruby and gold. It felt as though she was marching on the sunset.

At last she sat on a wooden bench facing a lake. The wind caressed her cheeks and the leaves rustled. She closed her tired eyes and sniffed the crisp air of autumn deep into her chest.

Yet the quietness lasted less than a minute. Too soon, her blank mind turned into a projector, showing a horror film: it was none other than her own movie, taking place last year, the worst time of her life. First, losing her beloved father and best friend to cancer. Then, her bitter divorce. Both bundled with endless stress at work. Last year's plagues flattened Grace to the ground, threatening to dig her grave.

"How long will this nightmare continue? Not a moment of rest," she grumbled to herself as tears gathered. Her blurry eyes stared at a young couple hugging and kissing.

There was a time when watching young lovers swirled butterflies of excitement in her stomach. Now, her abdomen turned into a dry log, idle to any hopeful sensation. Romance and love seemed impossible to her. Nothing more than a slippery dream offering an instant of hope, only to vanish forever. Better not to fancy than be disappointed, her guarded inner voice urged, pinching her heart time and again.

She rose to her feet and marched back to the car, blind to all the wonder around her. Her mind was so trapped in the sticky web of the past that she could see nothing of the magical present. Grace had no reason or will to celebrate her thirty-fifth birthday.

"Wake up, Luxrider...wake up..." A voice echoed under the milkweed plant.

Moments later, a twig vibrated. A crumpled butterfly broke through its chrysalis, emerging from its womb. Orange and black he was, with tiny white dots that fringed his wings like diamonds on a royal necklace.

Like a newborn baby who had just left the warmth and

safety of his mother, the stunned monarch blinked in the new light. Yet, rather than crying, he breathed for the first time and smiled at the morning sun.

His eyes idly scanned the juicy milkweed leaves. Only three weeks ago, fuzzy worm that he was then, he salivated and feasted on them nonstop, blind to everything else. But now that seemed nothing more than a far-off memory. Now his eyes wandered to the vibrant flowers and a new desire arose in his stomach. His virgin sucking tube unfurled for the first time, and his keen eyes grew wide.

"Juices of heaven..." he said, mesmerized.

Thrilled as he was, Luxrider still clung upside down to his old home, afraid to let go. His new wings felt like useless wrinkled paper as he tried to flap them in vain. Frustrated and confused, he held onto the last familiar thing he knew, the chrysalis.

"Is that all?" he wondered. "Long days of transformation so I would turn into a cripple?"

He scanned the new world with uncertain eyes. Now, it appeared frightening rather than exciting. *Perhaps*, he thought, *I can turn back into a caterpillar. At least then I would be able to survive.*

The crumpled monarch pushed his body up and attempted to squeeze back into his old shell. But he was too big.

"Ha-ha-ha-ha..." A roaring laughter sounded. "Already doubting yourself, Luxrider?"

The young butterfly lowered his eyes in shame. He recognized the voice at once. It was the same voice that had encouraged him in his dark hours of desperation and guided him into the light. The voice of the wizard of light.

"I just looked inside my old home..." Luxrider answered with innocent tone.

"Why? Did you forget anything?" The wizard teased him. "There is no going back, my boy; only forward. Today is your butterfly birthday. The old caterpillar in you must die before you can fly. Cast your fears and doubts aside and become who you were born to be. Flap your wings, my child..." his voice echoed.

"I am trying, but nothing happens," complained the monarch.

"Just keep flapping your wings..." the voice faded away.

Luxrider trusted the wizard's infinite wisdom more than he trusted himself.

He flapped his crumpled wings for long minutes, yet still nothing happened. He glanced around, hoping none were looking at him. He felt more ridiculous and stupid than an earthworm.

Suddenly, his little heart boomed. A fluid pumped from his body and flowed into his wings. They tingled now, and he slapped them together faster. Wonder of wonders, the four crumpled papers smoothed out into gorgeous, sturdy wings.

Luxrider studied his new flying tools with admiration. Not one wrinkle, not one crease. They were perfect.

"You are an idiot, Luxrider!!" he scolded himself, promising to never again doubt the wizard of light.

His empty stomach rumbled now and he craved some heavenly nectar. A morning breeze kissed him softly and he found himself rising a few inches, then landing back. He roared with a joyous laughter.

"Good morning to you, my dear butterfly," the wind whispered.

"Good morning," Luxrider replied in a hesitant tone. Up until now, the only voice he had heard was the wizard's voice.

"You shall ride on me whenever you wish. I am at your service," the wind said.

"Thank you," Luxrider answered.

A sudden beam of light caressed his wings, and the warmth spread throughout his body. The wind snorted.

"Move aside, young sister," said another voice, and the sunlight grew bright.

"Butterfly," said the wind, annoyed, "meet the sun, my older sister."

"Well, well, what do we have here?" said the sun. "This is no regular butterfly, sister, but a monarch of autumn, king of the butterflies. One who will embark on a miraculous journey."

Luxrider said nothing.

The wind remained still. Her older sister knew much about the world.

"The wizard mentioned something about a journey," mumbled Luxrider.

"Of course he did!" the sun snapped. "He is the wizard of light and wiser than all. Anyhow, I will warm your wings every morning and help guide you on your adventure. My light shall be your light. Three days from now, on my rise, look to the east and open your mind. Your journey will start then. Farewell for now."

"Happy birthday, Luxrider," called the wind and vanished with a blow.

The two sisters left, yet the monarch felt neither sad nor alone. He recalled the wizard's words: "You are surrounded by love, and the universe is your best friend."

With that cheerful memory and thought, Luxrider dropped his caterpillar life behind and flapped his wings. His body soared, and joy rushed through every cell.

"I am flying!" he screamed and laughed. "I am flying!"

And so he did. From tree to bush, he shifted the angles of his black-tipped orange sails. His empty stomach mooed like a cow, but he didn't care. All he wanted was to fly some more.

At last his wings gave up and he glided down like a dandelion seed, landing on a bunch of milkweed flowers.

Gazing at the pink petals bowing before a white crown at

the flower heart, Luxrider wondered how he'd managed to miss this magic before. As he rubbed his feet on the flower top, he sensed sweetness in his mouth. "Incredible," he whispered. At once, Luxrider uncoiled his sucking tube and sipped the nectar for the first time. A rainbow of sweet flavors gushed so fully through his body and mind, the young butterfly almost choked with excitement. Soon enough, he mastered his lively straw and penetrated more flowers like a professional driller.

At last he stood on the pink milkweed and tears of bliss trickled down his face.

"Thank you, my wizard, for not giving up on me. Thank you for showing me the light beyond the darkness," said Luxrider.

Moments later, he flapped his wings and fluttered in the garden—until he got caught in a spider's web.

When Grace arrived home, her hand trembled on the front door handle. Some days she found anger or bitterness inside; on other days, grief and loneliness. She pushed open the door, praying for the least painful emotion, whichever that was. Asking for peace seemed inconceivable.

She entered with hesitant steps and turned on the lights, yet no emotional thief lurked. A surprised smile curled her lips. She dropped her bag, took off her business suit and high heels, and donned colorful pajamas, thinking she might enjoy an afternoon nap. Then she had a brave thought. She rushed across the TV room, opened the sliding door and stepped out onto the patio.

A sudden wave of sadness smashed against her heart, and she almost fell to her knees. The intense sorrow didn't seem to come from within her but from the outside. As though the whole universe was grieving for something; as though a mother had helplessly witnessed the death of her baby.

From the corner of her eye something moved. She glanced to her right and noticed a spider's web.

The silk threads tied the monarch like iron chains. He tried to flap his wings, but they remained glued to the sticky trap. A swift shadow slid down on a string. It was a creepy brown spider with black marks on his back and legs. His jaws rattled with excitement, and his eight dark eyes grew wide.

"My wizard!!" Luxrider screamed in panic, but no voice answered.

"Wind... Sun... Please..." He tried to cry, yet a butterfly rarely shed tears.

The spider drooled as he got closer. His saliva stank like death.

"Why, wizard of light? Why?" the butterfly whimpered. "All the long days of transformation and suffering, just so I might sip nectar, fly a bit and die?"

"It is the way of the world, my child..." the wind breathed.

Her sister sun hid behind a cloud as death approached. She

didn't take sides. As much as she was for the monarch she had to also be for the spider.

"But I have so much to live for, to love and explore..." Luxrider sighed and turned his head from the advancing fangs, waiting for his inevitable death.

A sudden body of light approached, and the monarch's heart froze.

Through the dense silk, he caught a glimpse of a human hand. The fingers snapped the stunned spider away and cut his web. A moment later, they released Luxrider from the deadly trap.

"I knew you would save me, wizard of light! I knew it!" Luxrider flapped his cheerful wings and danced around the light. Then he landed on the savior's hand.

From his perch he gazed at a beautiful lady with hazel eyes and a smile that could melt a glacier in a second. "So it wasn't the wizard," he thought. Yet she glowed with the same light.

"Daughter of light, I am forever in your debt!" Luxrider said. Then he bowed and flew away.

For the first time in months, Grace laughed.

CHAPTER 2

A beam of light landed on Grace's bed. She blinked her eyes and gazed through her open bedroom window. Clear blue sky spread over the golden maples and the birds were singing a morning song.

She peeped at her watch. It showed 7:25 in the morning.

"Damn! I'm late," she cursed and jumped off the bed, rushing to the bathroom. After washing her face, she glanced in the mirror. Yesterday's red eyes had returned to their normal hazel tone, and the pillows that had plumped under her lashes had lost their padding.

"I needed that sleep," she sighed as she brushed her teeth.

After a quick shower, Grace opened her closet door. Like disciplined soldiers, the black and gray suits waited on the hangers, ready to impress and produce, ready to exhibit sharpness and efficiency. At the back of the wooden rod, colorful dresses and shirts hid behind the gray soldiers' column. She stared at them and her stomach twisted.

There was a time when Grace loved wearing turquoise and orange and emerald green. But now she felt much safer and predictable under the conservative gray and black masks. The artist within her, together with her vibrant personality, had died and become an ambitious attorney.

Although it was Saturday, and only her boss and a few others would be working at the office, she decided to go in. It had been two years since she had joined the prestigious law firm, but she still needed to prove herself in every way.

"You can always be better! You can always be more prepared," her boss told her. "This company breeds hardcore, relentless lawyers; only the winners survive."

"I'm a winner!" she announced to him.

"We shall see. The results never lie," he answered.

And so, like the other members of the firm, she became an extreme version of her serious self. Spinning in an endless storm, always striving to win and achieve. Soon clients and people became numbers, and cases counted only as wins and losses. In the midst of it, Grace lost balance in her life; her happiness came to depend entirely on winning and getting her boss's recognition. Yet, because of all the hardships she had suffered during the last year, the workplace became the only stable anchor in her shaky life.

Grace grabbed a black suit and dressed beside the window.

A patch of orange floated outside in the garden and landed on a flower; it sipped some nectar, and rose again. The lawyer gasped and chuckled. This must be the monarch she had saved. A warm sensation spread throughout her body as she followed the butterfly's path. He seemed so carefree and filled with life. *Only yesterday he was about to be eaten by a spider*, she thought. *Now, he is all happy and cheerful. I wish I could recover from a trauma so fast.*

The more she gazed at the monarch, the less she wanted to drive downtown. It's too beautiful a day to spend in a stuffy office, her rebellious voice whispered out of nowhere. Grace had almost forgotten its existence. With a mischievous smile, she tossed her business suit on the bed and put on navy blue leggings and an orange sweater. The high black heels remained in her room as she dashed barefoot to the kitchen, spoiling herself with a cappuccino.

Moments later, she took a book and her warm cup and sank into the patio sofa outside. The crisp morning air was as refreshing as a cool shower. She scanned the garden with admiration. The trees and plants appeared to be healthy and thriving. At last, a gardener who knows his job, she thought. Soon, she found herself deep into the book.

Luxrider flew around the backyard all light and happy. He practiced flapping his wings in all manners, diving and dipping and soaring and gliding. When he got tired, he rested and drank some more nectar from the neighbors' gardens. The terrifying spider incident had already faded. He was a monarch butterfly, after all, and his mind became as light as his wings. Fear didn't stick to him. Yet the desire to show gratitude to his savior stirred his heart.

He espied her from a distance as she lay on the sofa. When the woman closed her eyes and fell asleep, the lurking butterfly approached. For long moments, he glided in the patio, gazing at her. At last, he took courage and landed on her left cheek. Her eyelids twitched and stopped. Then, he placed his two antennae on her forehead.

Grace had fallen into a deep sleep when something flew into her dream. It was the butterfly from yesterday. Her hand opened up and a moment later the monarch settled on her palm.

"My name is Luxrider," he said. "I came to thank you for saving my life. How can I repay you, daughter of light?"

"Just be careful next time..." She smiled at him. "My name is Grace, not daughter of light."

"You are a daughter of light, Grace," he insisted. "You are all glowing with a golden light as bright as the wizard himself."

She gazed at him with puzzled eyes. "Wizard of light? Me? Glowing with a golden light? I think you need eyeglasses."

She laughed, but Luxrider didn't get the joke.

"We butterflies see light that you people cannot," he said in a serious tone. "If you could only watch yourself shining, you would change your mind at once."

At first, Grace said nothing. But something in the tone and certainty of his words grabbed her attention. "Who is this wizard you are talking about?" she asked offhandedly.

"He is one of you, the people of light. Yet he is a man like no other. His wisdom and kindness are beyond the world, and even the sun and the wind admire him. All butterflies know him as the wizard and sing songs of praise for him."

"Wow, he must be special," Grace said with a note of sarcasm.

"For us butterflies, he is much more than special. He is the voice of reason and hope, the one who accompanies us throughout our transformation. Before him, we had no hope."

Grace's mouth dropped open, for the butterfly's words stunned her. "How do you know all of this?"

Luxrider pumped his chest with pride. "While the rest of the butterflies sing him songs, we, the monarchs of fall, embark on a miraculous journey to his dwelling. Those of us who are fortunate enough to survive become his students. There, from the master himself, we learn about life and true love."

As the monarch said the words "true love" Grace's face turned sour and her smiling eyes frosted over. Her past failed relationships lashed out at her already-bruised heart, impelling her to snarl, "You are as naïve as a little boy, Luxrider. True love doesn't exist. Better for you not to start this stupid journey of yours, for you will be much disappointed."

"But...daughter of light, it must be true..." mumbled Luxrider, stunned.

"I have no light," Grace snapped. "My life is dark. Believe what you want to believe!" And she jerked the butterfly from her hand.

Luxrider pulled his antennae from Grace's forehead and flapped his wings as she opened her eyes. As he hung in midair, she rose to her feet. At last, she gave him a disturbed stare and dashed into her house.

"It was just a dream, Grace..." she whispered to herself and slammed the door.

CHAPTER 3

T he Sunday morning sun hadn't yet arisen, but Grace was already driving to the office. The streets were dark and quiet, and her competitive smile smirked. Starting the day early, before anybody else, made her feel productive. She grabbed a coffee from a sidewalk kiosk and went into the tall building. No one was inside except a sleepy security guard.

By 10 a.m. she had already studied her files, written her notes, and filled her notebook with a new to-do list.

For no apparent reason, Grace glanced out of the office window—and her skin tingled: high in the air, an orange and black butterfly passed by. Ten seconds later, two more monarchs flew behind him.

"Luxrider..." she whispered, and touched the glass with her hand. Words from yesterday's dream echoed in her head. "We, the monarchs of fall, embark on a miraculous journey..."

"It was only a dream..." She dismissed the voice and went

back to her desk.

However, she found herself reading the same sentences time and again. She couldn't focus anymore. Frustrated, she decided to return home.

Luxrider was gliding in the garden, yet his eyes searched for Grace. She hadn't come out to the patio since yesterday afternoon. Her words and harsh tone still sounded in his mind: "You are naïve as a little boy, Luxrider. True love doesn't exist. Better for you not to start on this stupid journey of yours, for you will be much disappointed." The monarch seemed confused and sad as he stood on a flower and stared at the patio door.

"What is it, Luxrider, not practicing your wings?" the wizard's voice asked. "Tomorrow morning you will be starting your miraculous journey. You should be ready."

"What is the point of this journey if true love does not exist?" muttered Luxrider.

"True love does exist, my child. But you must open your eyes and heart to witness it. Your journey will teach you much if you are willing to listen."

The monarch sighed. "I believe you, my wizard. It's just... when I heard the words of the daughter of light I got confused."

Luxrider told him about the conversation he'd had with Grace. While the wizard said nothing, the butterfly could sense his tense breathing.

"Why would a daughter of light be sad and bitter and doubtful?" Luxrider asked with a troubled voice. "Isn't she like you, my wizard?"

"She is like me in essence but she hasn't discovered her potential. She hasn't yet transformed. The glowing light around her is what she really is. Unfortunately, her dark mind doesn't let her see herself as such."

"Light her dark mind, my wizard," Luxrider said with a hopeful note, "the way you did with me. Without your support, I wouldn't have been able to transform."

"I tried many times, my boy," sighed the wizard, "yet my words and thoughts fell on deaf ears. People are different than butterflies. They are born with a naturally illuminated mind, but time corrupts it. Fears and guilt and anger and many other shadows creep in and take over. Soon enough, they build mighty walls of defense and place guards on them, keeping any hopeful thoughts outside. And so what is left of the bright mind is only a flickering candle flame, imprisoned, alone."

With these words, Luxrider sensed the warmth deserting his wings, and although butterflies seldom cry, he shed a tear. One single drop for the poor daughter of light who dwelt in the dark.

"Yet as long as there is flame there is hope..." added the wizard with an encouraging note. "Tomorrow, the sun will rise and you will start a journey like no other. Now go and practice flapping your wings some more, monarch."

Luxrider bowed respectfully and then soared into the air with a smile. He was a butterfly, after all, and sadness couldn't cling to him.

On her way home, memories of her beloved father flooded Grace's mind. Some were happy visions of her vigorous dad taking young Grace to school, or their long hours playing in the park. At each step in her life he was there, standing beside her like a mighty oak. So many times she leaned on his strong branches and encouraging words.

Moments later, images of him in the hospital came to her. Dressed in white and laying on his bed. His bony face and hollow eyes trying, without success, to force a smile. He had turned into half a man; the spark of life had abandoned him. Helplessly watching a lively person like her father decay and rot as though an army of termites were devouring him from inside, leaving only a gray, lifeless bark, was tearing Grace apart.

Tears flowed like rivers on her cheeks, and the road turned blurry. With a swift motion, she turned the wheel left and took a side street all the way to the cemetery.

Before she passed the brown iron gate, Grace stopped by the roadside and picked some pink flowers. Then she strolled along a path among trees and gray stones. The leaves on the ground stirred, and her gray business suit made a faint swishing sound as her arms brushed her sides. "I'm not so different from them," she thought, scanning the stones of the dead. "Just a walking grave."

At last, she reached her father's plot. It was her first visit since the funeral. She always seemed to have a reason or excuse for not coming. Now, she froze and stared at the cold stone. But when she bent to set down the flowers, her legs melted, and she dropped to her knees. In front of her the black letters read:

ROBERT COLIN

9.18.1951 ~ 8.16.2013

"All people die, yet only a few live."

She wept and sobbed for long minutes, draining rivers of pain through her eyes. When the grief for his loss had emptied, she was left with doubts and fears about her future. She cried again, this time for her miserable life.

Looking at the dull stone for help, she pleaded, "One last piece of advice, Daddy..."

But the stone said nothing back.

A monarch landed on the pink flowers she'd just picked and began sucking their nectar. A warm sensation grew in her chest, and her wet eyes twinkled.

"Do not ignore the omens in your life. They are here to show you the way," her father's words sounded in her head.

"That's right, Daddy," she wiped her tears. "'All people die, yet only a few live.'"

The butterfly flew away.
Grace rose and left her father's grave with a new spark.

CHAPTER 4

G race opened the sliding glass door and went out to the backyard. It was late and the sun had already started sinking in the west. A smudge of makeup ran under her eyes, but she didn't care. At last, after a year of delaying, she had finally confronted her fears and visited her father's grave.

Rivers of agonizing tears had drained away and lightened her soul, which felt now like a floating feather. Now she could enjoy the sight of her garden and the symphony performed by the birds. The monarch must have left, she thought sadly. But just as she turned back toward the house an orange butterfly flew by on her right. Grace smiled and held her hand out to him. Her heart skipped a beat as Luxrider made two swirls and landed on her palm. She gaped at him breathlessly, and a fluttery sensation raced in her belly.

"Is it possible he recognizes me?" she asked herself, sitting down on the patio sofa. The monarch remained glued to her hand and seemed to be staring back at her. Then, his two antennae moved and coiled around her finger like a wedding ring. A gentle vibration climbed up her spine to her neck and head; her soft skin turned into a sea of goosebumps. She couldn't move.

A slight shiver rushed through her again, and a voice spoke.

"Thank you for saving my life the other day," said Luxrider in a calm voice.

Utterly shocked, Grace just nodded. A moment later she found her tongue. "You came to me in my dream yesterday, didn't you?" Her lips quivered. "Am I crazy? Is this an illusion?"

"You are quite awake and glowing, daughter of light..." he said." Tomorrow I will leave for my journey only because of you."

Grace smiled. "Well, you must be more careful next time if you want your journey to last. The spider webs in the wild are thick, and the dangers are many."

Luxrider said nothing.

She went on and on, projecting her own doubts and fears. "A sudden rain could strike you down and a storm might smash you to the ground. In the sky, hunting birds are everywhere, and dragonflies and wasps might be on your tail. And anytime you land on a flower, a lurking praying mantis, a bug or a rat, might jump on you from his cover. Perhaps you should reconsider," she said with a caring voice.

"You are right, Grace; the dangers are indeed many. Yet, I will be on my way tomorrow, nonetheless."

"Wouldn't you prefer to stay in the neighborhood gardens? They are safer than the open fields, and the flowers and nectars are plentiful. Your chances to survive here are much better," the lawyer persisted with logically.

"If survival were my only concern, I would be born a spider or an ant, or even remain a caterpillar," said Luxrider. "But I am a wandering butterfly, a fall monarch, whose joy is the journey itself."

Grace lips parted, but she said nothing. This orange insect on her palm, weighing less than a paperclip, had silenced one of the most brilliant attorneys in Toronto.

"We butterflies do not dwell on fears from the past or what might go wrong in the future," he went on. "Instead, we live life to the fullest in the present, the only time that exists. Whatever happens in our journey, happens."

An uncomfortable sensation grew in her, and she swayed slightly on the sofa. Like deadly arrows, Luxrider's words had pierced her pride and self-image. As though he attacked her, she felt a need to defend her set of beliefs.

"Easy for you to say, monarch," snarled Grace. "What do you know about financial debt? A mortgage? Holding a job, or trying to keep a relationship? Nothing!! These are real hurdles, and with them come fears. We people have a much more complicated life than drinking nectar and flying from here to there."

Luxrider sighed. The wizard was right. Her mind built mighty walls of fears and doubts, blocking any light from entering. What a waste; such a shame.

He was about to flutter his wings and fly, but instead he said, "Close your eyes, daughter of light. I want to share with you a memory."

She gaped at him as he left her hand and landed on her head. As her stunned eyes looked up, Luxrider placed his antennae on her forehead. "Trust me, Grace. Close your eyes," said the monarch.

And she did.

At first, blackness filled her mind. Then there was a dim light which gradually grew brighter and she saw a blurry orange spot moving. Vague sounds followed. A moment later the picture cleared. A monarch butterfly sank on a milkweed leaf and laid a tiny white egg. Not on top but underneath, hidden from the eyes of predators. The egg was no bigger than the point of a penny nail.

Suddenly, the sounds became a soft voice filled with love. Grace shivered as though an angel was singing in her ears.

"My beloved son, here our ways are separated. I have no chance to see you blossom, nor to be a loving mother and warm you with my wings. I leave you to grow an orphan. But you are not alone, for love and light are all around you. Before my task is done, I bless you, my child. May the universe aid you on your path. May you survive and turn into a miraculous monarch."

A moment later, the butterfly flew away, and her song faded.

"Who is she, Luxrider?" Grace asked with a sad voice.

"It is my mother..." he replied.

Then, Grace sensed she was enclosed in an oval white balloon. Intense fears and anxiety pervaded the inside of the suffocating egg. The caged creature was hammering at the eggshell with his black head, yet couldn't come out. Anger and blame and fear filled the tiny space; there was no air left.

"Why did you leave me here? Mother! Mother!! Please, come back!" The voice cried and screamed and pounded his head again.

"Get me out of here! Luxrider! Get me out!" Grace shouted at once, and the monarch removed his antennae.

Tears rolled down her cheeks, and she gasped for air as though she had been underwater for a while. Moments later she stared at him as he landed on her hand.

"How long were you in that hell?" Grace asked in a trembling voice.

"Four long days, my lady..."

Grace's mouth fell open and she gazed at him with admiration. "How someone can survive such torture for so long," she wondered. She could barely handle the pressure for a minute or two.

"I knocked myself out of consciousness many times," Luxrider laughed. "Every time the leaf moved, my tiny home swayed—and I waited for death to come. Perhaps a bug or a spider was about to eat me alive. However, after passing through hell time and again, the fear lost its grip on me. Soon, I accepted my situation and struggled no more. In that first moment when my fear left me, I heard his voice—the wizard of light came to visit me for the first time."

Grace's eyes opened wide and Luxrider caught the hint. She was ready for more. He floated back to her forehead, upon which he placed his antennae. In a flash, she once again entered the little oval egg, joining the monarch's memory. He'd gotten much bigger now and was squashed against the walls of the shell. Nevertheless, it was very quiet inside. Suddenly, a beam of light penetrated through the white cover and for the first time since his mother left him, young Luxrider sensed love again.

"What are you waiting for, caterpillar?" a calm voice spoke. "Use your teeth."

"Is it the wizard of light?" Grace asked with awe.

"Yes," replied Luxrider.

"His voice is so..." She searched for the right word.

"Loving..." said the butterfly.

A moment later, biting the tasty eggshell, the newborn caterpillar had chewed his way out to freedom. He pushed and wiggled his body until a gust of fresh air welcomed his face.

"Ahhhh..."

The caterpillar and Grace breathed at the same time.

"It was so easy to get out..." Grace whispered in disbelief. "If only the wizard had visited earlier, you could have avoided that horrible experience." Her voice was filled with blame.

Luxrider laughed. "Fear and blame and anger filled my mind at first," he said. "But the wizard's voice comes to you mostly when you are ready for a change, or when you are calm. His loving guidance and light waited outside my egg, available to rush in and end the suffering. Yet my fears blinded me and blocked him from entering. Where fear is, love does not dwell."

Grace's heart saddened. "The wizard stayed right there, yet you couldn't hear him," she said and reflected on her own life. That had also happened to her. Every time she reached a crossroads with her career, a relationship, or even financial investments, she panicked. Only after a while, after the fear had dissipated, would an idea or creative advice from someone or just her inner voice come to her. Most of the time, the guidance that arrived was simple but brilliant.

She had been as blind as the newborn caterpillar many times and didn't see the light until the stress left.

"You are right, Luxrider," Grace said, and the butterfly smiled.

Perhaps he could help her after all.

The vision continued, and Grace found herself crawling with the baby caterpillar on the milkweed leaf. He was biting and munching and crunching and chewing day and night.

"It is unbelievable how much you can eat," she said, somewhat shocked.

"In two weeks I grew more than two thousand times my original weight," Luxrider answered. "Even though I ate nonstop, I was always starving. As my stomach expanded, so did my hunger. It felt like I had an empty hole, never to be filled."

"What's the point then?" Grace frowned.

"The wizard told me it was a necessary part of my growth. From the first moment I hatched out of my egg, I began eating. In my undeveloped mind, I was nothing more than a small, crawling bug. The more I identified myself with the caterpillar, the more my desire to eat increased. Long days and nights I consumed these leaves, asking no questions. Twelve eyes I had, yet I was almost blind, not being able to detect images around me. As I was ready to shed my skin for the fifth time, I halted. *Is this my life?* I asked myself. A never-ending craving that can't be satisfied? I'd had enough. *There is no point living like this,* I said to myself.

"At that moment, the wizard of light approached, laughing. 'Well, it's about time,' he said. 'I thought you would chew all the milkweed in the garden before you would realize that.' Then he instructed me to climb on the twig above, stick to the top and turn into a chrysalis. When I asked him why, he said, 'You are ready to transform.' 'Transform into what?' I asked, all puzzled. 'A butterfly! A fall monarch! A light rider!' he said with pride.

"'Me... a butterfly? It cannot be,' I said in disbelief. I used to watch them flying and singing and drinking nectar while all the bugs were gazing at them with envy and admiration. My timid and limited mind couldn't imagine that I might change into this heavenly creature.

"'There are no limitations except in your head,' the wizard said to me. 'Now climb and do as I say. Be brave and believe in yourself, and don't resist the process.'

"And so I did. Soon after, I stuck to a twig and stayed in my new home, rigid, like another part of the plant."

Grace sat speechless for long moments, digesting his words. She realized there was much more to this butterfly than meets the eye. Most of her life, she had thought of herself merely as a body, a piece of flesh and nothing more. Anytime someone mentioned something spiritual, she would say, "There is no more than what appears in the mirror." After all, she was a practical lady.

Yet now she began to question herself. The same as the caterpillar had asked himself, "Is that all there is to life?" Be born and grow, eat, live through pain and failure with only short glimpses of successful moments and pleasure. Become old and pass through illnesses and slow decay until you return to dust. Perhaps we are more than that, she now considered; perhaps life is meaningful and joyous. Look at Luxrider. Anytime he was present and not consumed by his fears, the wizard of light visited him. *I should try doing the same.*

A sudden image cut her thoughts and seized her mind. The frozen caterpillar pressed in his chrysalis. Any noise outside frightened him. His body squeezed so tight against the shell that he couldn't move a hair.

"I missed my days as a bug, eating in the fresh air," he complained. "Even in the egg I had more room than this. What am I supposed to do?"

Soon enough, the powerful jaws which had fed him in the past turned into an odd rolled tube. "No! Please, no! Why do you rip away my mouth?" he cried in panic and pain. "I will starve."

"So you shall feast on heavenly nectars," the wizard's voice answered.

Three days passed, and Luxrider screamed again. "Now you take from me my eyes. Now I will be totally blind!!"

"No, my child. Your two new eyes will show you a world like no other. Soon, you will see the light itself," the loving voice continued to encourage.

However when the caterpillar body split open to form wings, the screams were deafening, and the tears of pain gushed like a river. Even Grace wiggled like a worm on the sofa.

"It will be over soon, my boy," comforted the wizard. "Fears and doubts and anger must leave you before you turn into a butterfly. And when you do, your new wings will take you to distant lands and your mind will shine with love. Accept your change with a full heart."

With this last advice from the wizard, Luxrider disconnected his antennae from Grace's forehead, flitted to her lips, which he kissed softly, then flew back to her hand and wrapped his antennae around her finger.

Grace opened her eyes. Drops trickled down her face. She gazed at Luxrider.

"You are right, daughter of light," said the monarch with a soft voice. "I don't know about people relationships and stress at work, nor of financial hardships. But I do know about fears and anger and doubts. Yet now, I weigh a third of my caterpillar weight, for I shed my painful past. I will travel light in my journey."

"You are brave and wise, Luxrider," Grace smiled at him. "I wish I had a fraction of your courage and wisdom. May the universe protect you on your miraculous journey," she said without a hint of sarcasm in her voice.

At last, she sent him away and dashed inside. The most significant case of her career was about to start next week, and she needed to be nothing less than perfect.

CHAPTER 5

That night, lying in her bed, Grace was far from sleeping. She was sitting up, scanning her notes about the upcoming case. "I must win this trial, no matter what," her inner voice kept pressing as her body turned rigid.

Suddenly, Luxrider came to mind and her harassing voice turned silent. "The wizard of light doesn't visit while you are consumed with anxiety and fears." *I can hear one voice at a time*, she reminded herself. *Is it fear or joy? The choice is mine.*

Stillness fell on her. The chaos in her head ceased. Grace sensed the breath in her chest and the sound of the crickets chirping outside the window. Her eyes wandered over the white walls and dark wood floors, scanned the end table and her closet. She found herself smiling with wonder, as though she gazed at these things for the first time. No labels...no names... no past... All became fresh and alive in this quiet state of mind.

"This is the timelessness Luxrider meant... this is the

present." She sparkled with joy. "I want it to last. I don't want this feeling of peace to go away."

The moment she said that, fearful thoughts attacked and broke the calmness to pieces. Visions of what might happen this week if she didn't succeed swamped her mind. The whips of fears repeatedly lashed at her until she yielded to their will. Tears of frustration trickled down her trembling lips and her fingers clasped the pages. "I am nothing but a slave..." she muttered.

She went back to her notes and read, falling asleep shortly after, the reading light still glaring.

Luxrider woke up to the biggest day of his life. His little heart boomed like thunder. Dawn had just started painting the sky amber.

"A glimpse of a miracle to arouse a miraculous journey," he chuckled.

In the garden, no one else had risen. The monarch swayed restlessly on his leaf. His impatient eyes glared at the east, trying to rush the ball of fire. But the sun took her time and climbed at her own lazy pace. Every morning she decorated the heavens with various colors and shapes, making each sunrise like no other. She was an artist and couldn't be rushed in her task, for many creatures drew inspiration from her paintings.

"Come on...come on now..." Luxrider's antennae whipped

the air like a mad jockey. He needed to warm his wings, for without the sun's caressing rays, he was as good as a bug. Her loving light was as vital to him as nectar.

While the old sister crawled up, a sudden flash of light appeared at Grace's window. Without a thought, the monarch flapped his stiff wings and landed on the sill.

"I would have a glimpse of her one more time..." he thought, as he gazed through the glass.

Grace was sitting up in bed, staring at her laptop with nervous eyes. She bit her fingernails, scratched her hair and held her forehead with her palms. The daughter of light appeared anxious and worried as the new day rose.

Moments later, she rushed into the closet and, with a sigh, chose a gray business suit.

Luxrider's cheerful heart pinched. He had hoped yesterday's conversation would have helped her to grasp the light.

"Luxrider..." a soft voice whispered as the wind blew. "Ready for your big day?"

"I am..." He said, sounding much less enthusiastic than before.

"Fly to the maple branch, over there." The wind gave him a lift. "My sister is about to warm your wings and give you the sign."

He soared and landed where the sun already rested her rays.

"My wizard..." Luxrider whispered. He called a few more

times to no avail. Frustration plied his voice.

"He won't come, monarch. He sent me and the sun to wish you a successful journey."

"I need to speak with him, wind," said the butterfly. "Will you carry my voice?"

"To where?" the wind giggled. "The wizard of light is everywhere as well as within you. Ask with confidence and he will show up."

Luxrider cleared his mind from the sad image of Grace. "My wizard," he said with purpose and love.

A light spread around him and his wings vibrated in gratitude.

"Do you need a push or perhaps a blow to start?" the wizard teased the monarch. "I thought I would find you already on your way."

"I was ready and excited until I saw her," Luxrider glanced at the window.

"Not again, Luxrider. You can't help her, my boy. Just focus on your journey," the wizard said with a firm voice.

"Yesterday, I shared with her memories of my past. She heard your voice, my wizard, and I sensed a change in her. You must believe me."

The voice sighed and a silence followed. "There is a big difference between hearing and listening, butterfly," said the wizard. "My voice may have traveled through her ears but it was blocked by her suspicious mind. A real change won't happen as long as she dwells in her past and future. Last night I visited her, but she couldn't stay with me for long. Her flame is too weak," he mumbled.

"Yet as long as there is flame there is hope," Luxrider repeated the wizard's words. "Perhaps she needs to go on a journey in order for her to hear your voice," suggested Luxrider out of the blue. "Your wisdom and light gave me the courage to withstand an unthinkable transformation. It should do the same for her. If she can join me on my journey and reach the end, imagine the change she might have."

The sun stood still and the wind blew a whisper. The wizard remained silent.

"Do you ask me to transform her into a monarch, Luxrider?" he asked, and the words sounded strange even to him.

"She won't be able to go through this journey and remain the same, will she, my wizard?"

"No... she won't." the wizard muttered with a new realization. This three-day-old butterfly taught him something new.

"One thing, Luxrider. Grace must believe with all her heart she can transform—and she must desire it above all. Only then is it possible. If she doesn't agree, promise me you will embark on your journey with no weight on your wings."

"Thank you, great wizard. You have my word."

Luxrider zoomed to the window like an Apollo 11 spacecraft,

ready to share the exciting news with Grace. They were not to fly to the moon but to the depths of their souls, and Grace had a chance to be a pioneer of light among her people.

"Are you really going to let it happen?" the wind and the sun asked the wizard at once.

"My ladies," said the calm voice, "this morning, we are all Luxrider's disciples, for this young monarch has taught us a precious lesson of love. And, by the way, if a daughter of light chooses to transform into a butterfly, she doesn't need my permission to do so. All she needs is to know herself as the light, and everything will be possible for her."

Luxrider soared and dived around Grace's window, trying to grab her attention inside. However, she remained blind to his efforts and presence. She grabbed her leather bag and dashed downstairs, seeing nothing but the scenarios her mind fed her: the questions she should ask; the jury's and judge's responses. Grace imagined it all.

"I am here... come to the garden..." Luxrider pleaded as he stuck to the patio glass door. Yet again, she saw nothing and rushed through the front door out to the driveway.

The optimistic monarch didn't expect that to happen. He had been able to do the impossible and convinced the wizard of his way. But now, she left.

Without thinking, he floated high above the roof and sped to the front. Grace sat in her silver Mercedes, backing up to the street. Finally, she noticed him spinning outside the driver's window. She braked.

"Open the window, daughter of light..." he said.

She gave him a smile. "Good luck, Luxrider..." she said, and backed into the road. When she put the gear into drive, ready to accelerate into her mad life, he hovered in front. She turned her wheel left but the persistent orange patch held his ground, blocking her way.

Grace turned crimson. She had no time for this and couldn't be late for work. Not today. She shifted the gear to neutral and gunned the engine. More than three hundred horses neighed, but Luxrider stood bold and blinked not against the roar. She was about to charge her car forward when visions of the monarch's early life passed through her mind.

"What the hell, Luxrider? What do you want from me?" She kicked the door open and stepped outside. But the monarch had vanished. She searched the hood and the front yet found nothing.

Puzzled, she returned to her seat and drove ahead.

Soon enough, she forgot about the odd incident and her mind took over again. It was as automatic as the car transmission, navigating her through the streets while she was busy watching her projected movie, missing the reality outside. The trial's voices turned louder and the judge's face seemed sterner than before. She was about to lose the case and her heart boomed, ready to explode.

"Grace..." a voice called.

She scanned the imaginary courtroom, but no one was talking. She shook herself from her imaginings and peered through the car windows. The drivers at the traffic light seemed sleepy and uninterested.

"Down here..." the voice spoke again, and now she recognized it. On the forth finger of her left hand, where the wedding ring used to be, an orange monarch had wrapped its black antennae.

"What are you doing here..." she asked, puzzled. She turned the Mercedes onto a side street and opened the window. "You have a journey to go on. Fly now."

"I am here to offer you the chance of a lifetime, Grace. Hear me out." His voice was commanding and loving at the same time.

Grace found herself in silence.

And so Luxrider told her all about the conversation he'd had that morning with the wizard of light. "You must believe with all your heart that you can transform, and you must desire this change," said the monarch, repeating the wizard's words. "Only then, it's possible."

"I can't..." she muttered.

"Aren't you tired of living an empty life? The endless stress and grief and fears? Don't you want to learn another way? Cast away your fears, daughter of light. The wizard has given you a rare opportunity for transformation. You can become a butterfly and learn about happiness and joy!!"

"You don't understand! All the effort and dedication I've exerted just to be in the position that I am in now. Being part of the most prestigious law firm in Canada isn't something you can just dismiss. I can't leave on a journey and risk returning to nothing—if I come back at all."

"What is it worth to win fame and honor if you lose yourself on the way? Wouldn't you throw away all of that for a chance to find the power within you? To rediscover your glowing light and win happiness forever?" Luxrider asked.

Grace lowered her eyes in shame. She was paralyzed by the fear of loss and change.

"The wizard was right," said the monarch, disappointed. "People of light build walls of darkness in their minds and can't see beyond them. Who would believe that a useless caterpillar has more courage to change than a daughter of light? Goodbye, Grace..." said Luxrider. And he flew out of the car.

CHAPTER 6

G race watched the flying monarch until he vanished from sight. Emptiness and despair came over her as his last words kept playing in her head: "Who would believe that a useless caterpillar has more courage to change than a daughter of light?"

At last, she headed toward downtown and the firm. When she entered, the office was already a beehive of activity. Young interns with tense faces were rushing through the cubicles, trying to impress their superiors with their diligence. Of all, only one would have a future in the company, but not a life to himself.

At the end of the small offices, the conference room appeared. It was Monday morning, and the president pressed everyone with high expectations for the week. Through the glass, Grace noticed the unsmiling faces, all rigid and serious, tight as a bowstring. Pull a bit and the string would snap. *Is that how I look when I am there?* Grace wondered in disbelief. *So anxious and nervous?*

A sudden bitterness and sourness grew in her stomach, as though she had taken a hearty bite of a lemon, chewing the peel first and then going deeper into the acidy fruit. The office walls began to close in on her from all directions, threatening to coil around her slim body like a giant anaconda. She opened her mouth fully to grab at the air, yet just a thin trail of air came through. Cold sweat covered her face; her trembling knees could hold up no more. Images of baby Luxrider imprisoned in his tiny egg and not able to get out flooded her mind. With her last ounce of strength, she ran back down the hall and, burst out of the offices, gasping for breath. The elevator seemed terrifying, so she took off her heels and climbed down countless flights of stairs until at last she reached the parking garage and her car.

Never before had Grace suffered such a panic attack. Her forehead dripped beads of sweat onto the steering wheel; the air conditioner couldn't cool her off. Craving fresh air, she let down all the windows. Her foot pressed on the gas pedal, and the Mercedes raced through narrow streets and high-rises. "No more buildings," her inner voice screamed. "I need some open space."

In no time, she found herself at a nearby park. She got out of the car and drifted through the trees, then sank down onto the first wooden bench she came across. Tears gushed out, and she let them drop like waterfalls. She cared nothing more about anything.

"What is happening to me?" her voice trembled.

"You've begun to wake up, Grace," answered a voice.

At once, she jumped to her feet, wiped her face on her jacket sleeve, and glanced around. No one was there.

"Be calm, daughter of light," the loving voice spoke again.

"I know your voice," she mumbled, still searching around. "You are the wizard of light. The one who helped Luxrider."

"I am, Grace," said the wizard, and the wooden bench glowed.

She found herself attracted to this light. A gentle warmth began to wrap around her body as she sat down.

"It is a pleasure meeting you at last," he said.

"At last?" she repeated with wide open eyes.

"Well...I tried a few hundred times before, yet without success."

He roared with laughter as Grace's jaw dropped in disbelief.

"That's right, daughter of light, hundreds of times. I must admit, your walls of defense are quite thick and strong, almost unbreakable. Every time I attempted to get through, the gate was shut. Your mind shielded your light with much efficiency."

Grace was utterly silent for long moments. Only the birds sang, the wind whispered, and the rustle of leaves sounded.

Finally, she broke the silence: "Do I have a light within me?"

The wizard burst into laughter and the day grew bright. "You can light the entire world if you wish to do so," he said. "This is your true purpose."

Grace wore a doubtful expression on her face. "What about lighting my dreadful life first?" she said, almost dripping with sarcasm.

"Of course," the wizard said, "you need to find your flame first and realize who you truly are before you can light the world."

"What is this light you keep talking about?"

"It is joy, happiness, love...everything," said the wizard.

"And why," Grace asked, "did I hear you this time but not all those times before?"

"This time—at least for a moment—you finally let go. Your walls of defense collapsed. You questioned your life and reality so deeply; it flickered your inside flame and awakened the fire of change. Some people experience this after much suffering, others, in a moment of stillness and brilliance. Now it's your decision, daughter of light. You may dismiss my voice and return to your hectic life with all the emptiness and fears and doubts. Or you can strengthen this experience and turn the spark of change into an infinite fire of transformation, forever to illuminate you and the world."

Grace's heart boomed. She recalled what Luxrider had told

her that morning. "Is it true I can turn into a monarch and go on a journey?" she asked.

"Yes, my daughter. It is a journey like no other. For the wandering monarchs are the masters of change. If you reach the journey's end, you will transform and never be the same. Then you shall share your knowledge and experience with your brothers and sisters and bring light to the world."

"And if I fail to reach the end?"

"You will die. But at least you will have been on a miraculous adventure. How many people can say that? What's more, when an autumn monarch dies on his travels his glowing image remains at the same place. The dead butterfly turns into a shining stepping stone, guiding and encouraging his brothers to continue their journey. Death might serve a purpose also."

On hearing these words, walls of fear and doubt arose in Grace's mind, hiding the light. The warmth of the wizard started to leave her body. Her inner voice warned her: "You will die for certain!" Her fearful voice spoke: "So many dangers and risks outside. You are not a butterfly. Perhaps in the future you can try, but not now. You are not fit for such a thing." As the dark voices grew, so the walls climbed higher. From the flame of change within her, only a dancing shadow remained; soon even that would be hidden.

The wizard's loving voice faded into a last whisper: "All people die, yet only a few live..."

Grace's heart froze and the hair at the back of her neck rose like porcupine spines. An image of her beloved father's grave appeared. That faint murmur smashed the walls in her mind like a powerful hammer, leaving not one stone standing. Her hazel eyes gleamed with new light, turning into melted gold.

"My wizard!!" she shouted, "I am ready for a new adventure!"

"Indeed, my child..." The wizard's calm voice spoke clearly from within her, forcing the doubts away.

Grace sensed her body vibrating as though she was a giant violin and someone had pulled the strings with all his might. A flash of blinding light struck, and she closed her eyes.

"May the blessings of the universe be with you and the light show you the way..." the wizard said—then vanished.

Grace opened her eyes and almost choked. She could see all around her at the same time. Not only that, but the world had turned into a feast of colors she had never seen before.

Everything appeared gigantic now. Maple trees were glowing skyscrapers. Birds were colorful jets. Giant people glowed, some in gold, some purple, others red. The wooden bench beneath her was as big as a horseracing track.

"Ride on me, Grace," the wind laughed and blew the monarch into the air.

At first she drifted like a clumsy piece of paper, lacking control and grace.

"Flap your wings," instructed the wind.

She did. After a few dips and rises, she managed to fly, and her joyous screams filled the park. Soon the wind guided her to a small lake nearby. Grace glanced at the shimmering water and her heart sang. An image of a gorgeous monarch reflected on the lake's surface. She dived closer to investigate and realized it was she. Admiring herself, she squealed, "I am a monarch butterfly!"

With a mischievous smile, she unrolled her straw-like mouth and let it skim the water.

"Indeed, your grace," whispered the lake.

For the first time in her life, Grace loved herself and felt beloved unconditionally.

CHAPTER 7

A nd so Grace flew through the air, free like never before. No gray suits, no tight schedule, no to-do list.
Even gravity barely affected her as she floated on the
wind like a cottony white cloud, clear of gray smears and past
memories. All that was left to her was the pure present moment;
nothing else mattered.

The world seemed so magical to Grace; her attention flowed
fully outside. Four orange sails navigated her ship through new
waves of colors and perceptions, igniting her butterfly's mind.
No grinding thoughts or disturbing voices bothered her. She
found herself soaring on the warm wind with no effort at all.
Tall buildings spread beneath her orange wings and the breathtaking sight sent her heart into spasms of joy. "It's great to be
alive..." she caught herself crying over and over as Toronto dis-
appeared behind her. Up there, more than a thousand feet high,
the quietness became unreal. Only the wind breathed.

All of her life Grace had been terrified of being lonely. Eating in a restaurant by herself or going to a movie without company seemed inconceivable. Now she was completely alone, yet far from being lonely. In utter solitude, she glided between earth and sky, not craving anyone beside her.

Once the extreme elation passed, peacefulness and serenity she'd never experienced before cocooned her heart.

Colorful fields and woods glowed beneath her. She started to crave nectar.

At that moment, she heard a distant song. The sound was softer than the fluffy clouds above her. Perhaps these are angels singing, she thought, and glanced on high. Grace found the blazing sun instead.

"No angels here, daughter of light," the sun chuckled. "Why don't you look down..."

Grace started to dive. The fields grew large, and the delicate voices became clear. She scanned the ground with puzzled eyes yet discovered nothing.

"These are the wildflowers, singing for you," said the sun.

"For me? But they don't know me..."

"They scan the sky for orange wings and when they see a monarch, they sing."

"Why?"

"They desire your touch, your presence, your blessings..." answered the old sister.

Grace seemed confused. "My blessings? But I am just a butterfly," she said.

"Don't underestimate yourself, my child. Everybody in nature knows the monarchs of fall are magical. Some name you the miracles carriers, others the light riders. No other creatures embark on such a journey to discover the essence of life and true love. Only the monarchs of fall have been chosen to become students of the wizard of light."

Grace pondered the sun's words, and her heart pounded with pride. *Who would guess the monarchs were so special? I am so fortunate to have met Luxrider. I wonder where he is. I hope all is well with him.*

Soon after, she thanked the sun for her guidance. A butterfly always gives gratitude to all along his way. That's why blessings and help keep coming to him.

"Here comes the glorious monarch

Flying on its miraculous journey.

Come and enjoy our heavenly nectar

And share your wisdom and blessings."

Grace unfurled and furled her long straw mouth in utter shock. The colorful fields of daisies were singing as one, swaying their heads in the wind. She chortled and landed on a yellow one. The sweetness zoomed through her legs up to her head. At once her tube drilled the flower's heart, sucking and drinking.

The flavor was paradise. It reminded her of a mix of berry

juice only a hundred times better. She jumped to a white daisy and drank some more, trying to please as many as she could.

Suddenly, something shook to her left. Grace withdrew her straw and focused on a plant. A dead monarch tangled in a web. Only one bitten wing remained. Ten inches above, a black and yellow spider lurked, his long, sharp legs extended like lethal spears. He stared at her with bloody eyes.

The nectar sprayed from her mouth as she flapped her wings in panic and fled from the flower. Terrible fear rushed through her, and she trembled in midair, staring at the deadly trap. "That could be me..." she shivered, "that could be me..."

At once, the flowers, stunned, stopped singing and swaying. They were not used to seeing a monarch behave like this. Instead of the sweet scent of joy, sourness spread from her body. She smelled like a frightened bug.

Grace continued to fly southward, but the image of the ripped butterfly haunted her. And while she desired to drink more delicious juices, she didn't dare to take the risk. "It's much safer here..." she convinced herself.

The sun was sinking in the west, painting the sky gold and red. Grace kept flying.

"You stink of fear, monarch," the sun's voice, like her colors, faded. "Time for you to rest until tomorrow."

"My sister is right, Grace," the wind followed. "Butterflies fly when the sun is out. You should find a place to perch soon."

"No...no need to stop," Grace said in an anxious voice. "I can fly to the end of my journey without a break."

The wind roared with laughter. "It's a long journey, my child, of many days and nights. You must rest."

Out of breath and words, the monarch landed on a pine tree.

"Good night..." said the breeze and left her on a lonely branch.

Her stomach growled with hunger. She sensed the exhaustion in her shaken body. Darkness crawled over the land and every sound made her heart jump.

"What have I done?" she said with horror and gazed at the starry sky. "What did I think to myself? I am not a butterfly."

All of a sudden a star glinted and before she knew it Grace sensed the wizard's warmth.

"Your neighbors downstairs complain of your rumbling stomach!" he said. "And, by the way, the rats around here smell fear from far."

Grace neither smiled nor laughed.

"What is bothering you, daughter of light?"

"I have orange wings and I sip nectar, yet I am far from being a monarch. What am I, wizard?"

The wizard sighed. "You are a butterfly, Grace, yet your mind is split."

"What do you mean?"

"Every monarch goes through a transformation when he

leaves the caterpillar life behind him and turns into a butterfly. In that process, not only the body changes but also the mind. Past fears and pain are drained out; what's left is the butterfly's mind. When you turned into a monarch, your body changed, yet you kept your old mind with you," explained the wizard.

"I would never survive like that," she snapped. "You may as well throw me into a spider's web or to a rat so I will have a swift death."

"Calm down, Grace!" The wizard's voice turned firm. "This is the purpose of your journey. You shall experience everything with your old human mind as well as with the monarch's new mind. By journey's end, your mind will be one and powerful. The journey is your transformation, so embrace each part of it."

She pondered the wizard's words for a while, and the fear started to leave her at last.

"Thank you, my wizard," said Grace and she fell into a deep sleep.

CHAPTER 8

"Wake up, sleepy," rustled the morning breeze, "time to meditate."

Grace opened her eyes and yawned. A new dawn was rising in the east, shedding the heaviness of yesterday.

"Let me sleep..." she complained. Her wings felt as rusty as an old machine. "I am still cold."

The wind gusted through the pine branches and the monarch found herself spinning up and up until she landed high on the tree's crown.

"A butterfly doesn't wait for things to happen!" the wind rebuked her. "He makes things happen!"

Now, she was fully awake. The first rays of the day tingled her, and Grace felt rejuvenated. Soon, the sun had brushed the rust off her wings, and her motor roared, set to roll.

"All right, I am ready for another day!" she announced in a

determined voice.

Grace flapped her wings and rose above the tree when a strong wind came along and pushed her back down to the top branch.

"Why are you doing this?" she snapped at the wind with blazing eyes.

"This isn't the way a monarch begins his day, daughter of light," said the wind. "People wake up, grab their coffee and race out for another hectic day. Later, they are surprised nothing goes their way. Don't you think I watch your ways of life?" the wind said.

Grace opened her mouth to reply but instead said nothing.

"You won't survive long, keeping your old habits. Listen to our teachings and open your monarch mind. Soon enough, you will bring miracles to wherever you go."

"Miracles?" Grace mumbled in wonder.

"Yes, miracles, daughter of light. While your human mind mostly focuses on problems and limitations, the golden mind of the monarch sees possibilities."

The wind is right, she thought. *I chose this ride, and I should learn to open my eyes.*

What is the use of a journey if I still act like the old me? "Very well..."

The wind sensed a shift in Grace.

"Where were we...? Oh yes... How a monarch begins his

day?" said the wind. "The reason I woke you up at dawn before the sun was out…"

"But I cannot fly until my body is warm enough, can I?" Grace cut her short.

"True," answered the wind. "Yet you need to prepare your mind nonetheless. A monarch regards every day as a small journey. He wakes up with the same excitement he had on his first day, curious about new possibilities and experiences."

"I know what you mean," said Grace. "I always prepare myself for a business meeting or a task ahead of time."

"Being prepared for a task and activity is helpful. However, I speak about quite a different preparation. A mental tuning."

Grace's mouth fell open.

The wind explained. "While his wings are not ready to fly yet, the monarch sinks into stillness to reach the miraculous realm."

"What is this realm?"

"It is a state of mind where one experiences the truth."

"How do I reach the truth, my wind?" Grace asked with glinted eyes.

"You don't reach it by going to a place, for it dwells within you at all times. However, it is cloaked in many layers. Blankets of old beliefs and ideas block your access. The monarch calms his mind, watches nature wake up, and listens to the morning sounds. Soon, he senses only the present—and becomes one with it. Not before that moment, when he enters the miraculous state of mind, does he embark on his day."

"I thought I should focus on my journey's end, on the results only," the lawyer's voice spoke. All her life was about achieving the next goal and reaching the next step.

"As I said before," the wind replied, "you need to open your monarch mind to experience a miraculous life. When the results of the journey's end are the only things that matter, your attention is often in the future."

"Is that so bad?" Grace asked.

"Well... It's not that it is bad. It's just that it's an illusion. The future is only a possibility of something that might happen. Your mind creates it. Being at some imaginary point in the future, you miss your present life, your journey, and growth. The truth exists only here and now. The main reason most people don't find it is because they search in the wrong realm and the wrong time."

Grace gave a sigh. "So much time I dwelled in the future or in my past...while missing my life."

"It's a disease worse than any other, my child," said the wind. "People work, eat, drink, and live as though asleep. They dwell in their memories and jump into an imaginary future. Living in the present, the only true reality, is quite rare among your people."

"What is the cause of this? How can we live differently?"

Grace asked.

"Your human mind is complex, filled with voices, ideas, and labels. It can turn into a monster, controlling you rather than you controlling it. Sooner than later, the mind becomes your master and you lose your essence. The only way out is to regain the mastery of your mind. Become a monarch, Grace, and you will transform."

"Too much information for one day, sister," called the rising sun. "Time to fly, little one!"

"Thank you for your wisdom, wind," said the monarch and flapped her wings.

Grace flew only a few miles before her empty stomach could hold no longer. "I must drink some nectar..." Still, images of the spider harassed her.

"Become a monarch, Grace," she said to herself. "Disregard the fears. They exist only in your head."

She dived into the fields and found a few blue harebells and some pink and yellow lilies. The area seemed clear of any hunters and so she feasted on the flowers' nectar. With her stomach full, she soared again, satisfied with the rich breakfast but mostly of facing her fear.

Towns and villages sprawled on the green land under her wings. She marveled at the blades of grass and the many kinds of trees. Cars were racing on the gray roads and people crowded the main streets.

Grace, the monarch, felt totally in the present. Her fresh eyes found the beauty in all, beyond their limiting labels. Soon, peace filled her mind and no voice interfered.

"That's what the wind meant," Grace chuckled to herself. "This is the joy of the now. Nothing is alike."

And so the butterfly floated as low as the treetops, singing and sipping nectar as she desired. "This journey is not so bad after all," she said with renewed confidence.

A moment later something shined in the distance. Almost blinded by it, Grace flew toward the glowing surface. It appeared like an infinite golden mirror spreading from east to west and far into the south. Beyond the gigantic reflection, she saw nothing.

"The grain fields are shimmering like a gold blanket," she mumbled with awe and excitement. But when she reached the edge of the glowing surface, she found no stems, no leaves, no golden wheat heads. A vast sparkling lake was all that she gazed upon, and it spread beyond the horizon.

"The Great Lakes..." her voice lost all its cheerfulness. "I can't cross this endless water."

The hour grew late. She found a tall red maple to roost for the night. Soon after, the sun was setting, coloring the sky and the lake in orange and pink. The flaming maple leaves turned into precious rubies highlighted with a spot of monarch amber.

"Incredible sight, isn't it?" the wind swirled through. "My

older sister is a true artist. I am more the practical one."

Grace smiled. The breathtaking view seemed like a perfect picture.

"You did quite well today, butterfly," said the wind.

Okay, but what should I do now? How the hell I am going to continue from here? Grace's old doubtful voice spoke inside her. Aloud, she said, "Thank you." Then she thought, *the wind has told me to accept the present time with any situation it brings. I choose not to complain, for complaining is resisting what already exists.*

At that moment, the troubles of tomorrow's challenge dissolved into the colorful lake. What remained was the peacefulness and beauty of the now.

The wind gasped with admiration. This monarch is a swift learner, she thought. Then she said, "Now, it's time for the sunset practice."

"Sunset? I thought preparation was only at dawn. What do I need to prepare for if I am about to sleep?"

"Sunset time is not for preparation but growth. At the end of a day's journey, relax and quiet your mind. Look at the lessons you learned and give gratitude for everything you have experienced."

Grace took a deep breath. "Even the bad experiences?" she asked, as she didn't see how these might help her.

"Bad for one is good for another. These are all interpretations and points of view. It was bad luck for the monarch to be trapped in the spider's web, yet a good meal for the spider. Whatever happened should happen. A monarch embraces everything on his way and learns from all. That is why the universe embraces him back and provides him all the blessings."

Grace closed her eyes and breathed. Moments later, her mind dropped into profound tranquility. She was thankful for the nectar on which she dined and the spectacular scenes she beheld, for the flowers' songs, the wind's wisdom and the sun's warmth. Soon enough, she found herself giving gratitude for unfavorable events as well. She thanked her hungry stomach, which forced her to confront her fears and feast on the flowers again. Even the creepy spider no longer appeared like a monster but a creature who tried to survive like everybody else.

Now she opened her eyes and gazed at the vast purple lake. His sight raised fear in her no more. He was a lake. Neither good nor bad. A challenge she had no idea how to overcome, but would face tomorrow nonetheless.

"I'm beginning to feel the change in me..." Grace's eyes sparkled with joy.

"Good night, monarch," laughed the wind, and the red maple leaves rustled.

CHAPTER 9

D usk turned dark and the night grew old. Among the maple leaves an orange light glowed. The wizard came to visit the young monarch, but she slept like a log. He gazed at her and smiled. The wind had spoken the truth; a transformation was starting to take place. He caressed her wings and left.

At dawn, Grace was already awake. For years, she hadn't sleep well. Now she felt as fresh as the grass under morning dew. The golden rays stroked her as she dived into a deep stillness. Her mind turned calm.

But then a sudden memory of the endless lake emerged, arousing thoughts and doubts.

Where is the wind? How am I going to cross this lake? Her voice urged, disturbing the peace in every possible way. Frustration started to build up in the monarch as the voice took over.

"Open your eyes, daughter of light," said the sun. Grace

gazed ahead and gasped in awe.

"It's beautiful..." she whispered.

The sun laughed. "I made it for you. Look to the east."

Grace stared to her left. The sky was painted orange above the silver lake. Some thin lines of scattered white clouds bordered the orange patch and shaped it like...

"A monarch..." said Grace in wonder.

"It's you, my daughter," the sun smiled at her stunned face. "Now look at the lake. What do you see?"

"He is calm and pristine," unlike my mind, she thought.

"True. The lake is a perfect mirror when the water is still. Clouds, birds, and the heavens enjoy their reflections on his surface. Yet one ripple is enough to distort the mirror and twist the images on the water."

The sun is speaking in riddles, thought Grace. *Not like her younger sister*.

"I must clear my mind of thoughts...of ripples...so I might see reality flawlessly," she realized out loud.

"Sharp as a razor," said the sun with a content voice. "At dawn, be still like the lake. No animal drinks from him, no birds hunt yet and the fish are all asleep. None disturb his peace."

The old sister's images were quite vivid, and her message struck the butterfly like waves of wisdom. Grace needed that extra advice to help her master her rebellious mind.

"But what happens when dawn passes and the animals

agitate the water and even the wind blows ripples? What shall I do then?"

The sun turned silent, and the sophisticated lawyer's voice in Grace's head smiled in victory. It's all good in theory, while everything is calm, the voice insisted. Yet, life always throws in some challenges and difficulties. How do you keep your stillness then?

"You dive like a whale..." answered the sun.

"You what?" Her arrogant voice startled and trembled at the same time.

"Ripples and waves, rain and storms, disturb the shallow surface and the lake's appearance, but never his depth. Deep under, stillness exists, no matter the force of the wind or the height of the waves. Whatever the situation outside, he remains calm. From the depth of his soul, the lake is able to watch the storming and violent surface, understanding it's not him. It's just a temporary disruption that will pass."

The lawyer's voice became mute as though sharp pincers had uprooted its tongue. It was no match for the wisdom beyond thoughts, where the realm of miracles exists.

"So the secret of remaining calm and mastering stillness under disturbing conditions is not to identify with the situation," Grace said out loud.

"That's right, butterfly!" the sun cheered. "Sometimes thoughts storm into the mind from nowhere and carry with them the seeds of anger, guilt, and fear. Dwelling on these thoughts turns a spark into a raging blaze, one that burns you from within and makes life into a living hell. That is why it's so vital to guard and master your mind. You must become the keeper of your garden, nourishing the seeds that grow into flowers and uprooting the ones that evolve into thorns. Soon enough, you will become the silent watcher, the one who observes her thoughts and emotions calmly. By understanding they are not part of your essence, you create a golden canyon that separates the light within from the negative thoughts and emotions that try to pull you into darkness. In such a miraculous state of mind, you will see the truth despite the storm."

Tears dropped from Grace's eyes. She realized how much suffering and pain she could have avoided if someone had told her this long ago. "Perhaps someone did," she thought, "but I wasn't ready to listen. I brought unnecessary drama and misery on myself."

"The past is gone and what's left is the present," said the sun. "Remember, butterfly, turmoil and tension occur only on the surface. They can suck you in and mix you with them until you forget who you are. But if you grasp the truth they have power neither to disturb you nor pull you into darkness."

Remembering the sun's inspiring art at dusk and dawn, she sighed, then spoke: "I always judged artists as dreamers and impractical people, but your art is wisdom that kindles the heart and rouses the sleepy mind. I recognize your words as the truth," said Grace.

"You recognize what you already know," said the sun. "Time to apply what you learn, butterfly. When in doubt, gaze at the lake and you shall remember this lesson."

Grace bowed to the wise sister and closed her eyes. She could see herself at the bottom of the lake. All became quiet. All turned still.

Sunrise dissipated the chill of dawn and the monarch opened her eyes and soared. She landed on a nearby flower on the lake's bank and drank nectar. To her surprise, the flowers neither sang, nor whistled, nor swayed. They appeared quite frozen and lifeless. Their heavenly juices tasted earthly and ordinary. Even slightly bitter.

"What is wrong?" she spoke to a few of them. "The graveyard flowers are more cheerful than you."

None of them laughed. A strange sensation ran through Grace as the tense silence continued.

At last a young flower with a sad voice spoke: "Must you fly over the water, monarch?"

"Yes, little daisy. My journey lies beyond the lake," smiled Grace.

The little daisy bowed and said nothing more.

A moment later, a large daisy swayed between them. "Forgive my son, butterfly; he didn't mean to dismay you. May the blessings of the universe be with you."

Although the larger daisy tried to hide his unease, Grace picked up on the note of anxiousness in his voice.

"All right now," she said, "what is going on? Why are all of you flowers acting strange and tasting sour? Is it me you don't like?"

"No, monarch," sighed the big daisy. "Do you really want to hear why?"

Grace nodded, but her heart raced.

"We are the flowers that grow on the lake's northern bank and so are the first to receive rumors and news from the water. Many monarchs feasted on our juices before they flew south. Every morning we blessed them with songs and food, yet by dusk the ripples of the lake carried grave news."

Grace swallowed a drop of bitter nectar, afraid to hear more.

"Most of the monarchs who pass by us find death on the vast lake," the big daisy said mournfully. "Their miraculous journey ends in the icy water. Because we witness so much demise, our laughter turned into whimpers and our songs into lamentations. Now, we prefer to be silent and encourage no more butterflies to die."

Grace panted as though she had raced up a steep hill. Bad news indeed. "Why has no one told me about this?" she muttered with a blaming note.

The flowers began whistling a sad tune, and the monarch's

light waned like a moon cloaked by a cloud. Then she remembered the stillness at the bottom of the lake. She flapped her wings and soared above the endless water. "I don't care about chances. I will make it through!" she shouted.

For hours Grace flew, yet no sign of land appeared on the horizon. She beat her wings when she had to and glided on the soft wind whenever she could, to conserve her energy. And although her strength dwindled, the peaceful lake calmed her mind and reinforced her resolve.

Suddenly, glowing bright spots flashed in midair. Some were in front while others to her right. Grace drew nearer and discovered they were the marks of dead monarchs, sparkling and frozen in midair.

"When an autumn monarch dies on his journey, his glowing light remains at the same place," the wizard had once said. "A dead butterfly turns into a shining stepping stone, guiding and encouraging his brothers to continue their journey."

But the more glowing monarchs she passed, the deeper Grace's despair dug into her heart, leaving not one cell of bravery there.

"So many...so many died here..." her voice trembled. Rather than finding encouragement in their light, she only saw hints of what the gloomy future held for her. The desperate words of the flowers on the bank echoed in her mind, turning each hopeful thought into a dark shadow that soon grew into a shivering lamentation of her name. Panic seized her. Her orange wings shivered. Ahead, the glowing path of death grew wider. Grace sensed darkness creeping over her. She shrieked, turned back north and flapped her wings furiously, as though an eagle was on her tail.

In the late afternoon, she collapsed beside the flowers on the northern bank. Exactly where she started. She fought for each breath like a racehorse. Her stomach was no thicker than a leaf. Not one drop of nectar or a bit of strength was left in her.

The sad flowers recognized her and started to sing and laugh and whistle. One less monarch to cry for. They swayed their heads and offered her to come.

"Don't get close to me!" she snarled in fury.

The singing flowers became mute and stiff. They didn't understand.

"Your nectar is poison to a monarch. All your sorrow and fears raised my doubts and snatched my mind at my weakest point. I would better starve than feast on your bitterness again."

The harsh words stabbed the delicate flowers. "We didn't mean to weaken your purpose," said the flowers on the bank. "We just shared the sad news..."

With no strength to fly, Grace leaped like a cricket. "You are the flowers on the bank. Our last stop before we fly to a challenging part of our journey. You, of all your flower brothers, have the biggest responsibility to fulfill your purpose and encourage us. Yet instead of singing happy songs to raise our spirits and wings, you offer us sad lamentations. Your sour nectar is crammed with doubts and pulls us to our graves. In this impossible marathon, a monarch will perish if he lets fear seize him."

With that said, she left the stunned flowers behind and, despite her exhaustion, headed to find some others inland. At last, she found flowers with nectar sweeter than honey.

Grace feasted until her paper thin stomach inflated into a balloon. Sunset approached, and she returned to the precious maple tree with its ruby leaves. The hard lessons of the day seared her mind like a red-hot blade on flesh. Reflecting upon them, a sense of calmness came over her. As the sun sank, so her mind followed into the stillness of the lake.

"Tomorrow is another day..." Grace sighed to herself. Her tired eyes felt like weighty gravestones. She couldn't even open them to appreciate the painting of the sunset. And so she sank into a bottomless sleep.

CHAPTER 10

D awn had only begun to spread its warmth, but the monarch already stood on her feet, her body recovered from yesterday's grueling experience. In case the sun and the wind questioned her, she rehearsed the excuses she would offer for having turned back. Yet neither of the two sisters spoke to her; nor did the wizard visit. Despite her troubled thoughts, she managed to practice the monarch's dawn meditation.

I don't need the sun nor the wind and the wizard to pat my back, she realized. *It is my journey and my lessons to learn. I should do my best for my own sake and accept no excuses.* At last she opened her eyes and bowed to the soaring ball of fire in the east. Her wings soaked in the loving rays. Moments later she left the tree in search of a sweet breakfast on the inland flowers when she heard laughter and singing from the lake. Curious, she turned and looked down. The flowers on the bank were swaying and crooning in harmony and with such love that the monarch's wings flapped and pulled her to them.

"No!" her human voice spoke. "Remember yesterday, their sour nectar and saddened songs. You made a promise not to visit them again."

For a few moments, she hovered in midflight, her butterfly heart pulling her down toward the flowers while her harsh human voice kept her away. She glanced at the tranquil lake, and her spirit grew bold. A beam of light shooed the old voice away.

"The bitter flowers on the bank have changed..." Grace's eyes glinted. "They rediscovered themselves. Who am I to judge them for yesterday's actions? I shall be the first one to embrace them for their courage and transformation."

Love and forgiveness inflated her heart and she sprang toward the lake.

"Good morning, pretty flowers," she said and landed on one.

The flowers laughed like little children, happy and light and carefree. She sipped their nectar and found it heavenly.

"You showed us the light, Grace, thank you," said a yellow daisy.

"I didn't do anything, except become angry with myself," said the monarch humbly.

"You are wiser than you think," bowed the flower. "For long generations, the flowers on the bank had been considered the black sheep among our brothers. Dwelling beside the water, the ripples constantly brought us news of the grave loss of the wandering monarchs. Soon enough, we became so dependent on this death news, we craved more. Happiness, singing, and love seemed like a distant dream as we forgot our natural-born purpose. Yesterday, you awakened us from a long, dreadful nightmare. You reminded us of our lost meaning and evoked a forgotten light. Your wisdom turned our bitter nectar into honey."

Grace stood speechless. She hadn't transformed herself yet seemed capable to change others. Her light radiated on the flowers as she joined their songs.

"The flowers on the bank will share no more bad news. We are forever in your debt, Grace of the monarchs, and will sing your name until the end of time."

Now her stomach was filled with nourishing food. Her wings became lighter than the wind. *Nothing will stop me from reaching the other side,* she promised herself. After this miraculous morning, her confidence and light skyrocketed. The morning breeze helped her much more than yesterday, and she glided effortlessly above the shimmering water. Grace sang the flowers' song and joy flooded her heart.

"Life is magical..." she cried and the lake chuckled with her. The glowing monarch stepping stones came into sight yet didn't disturb her at all. Her mind became as still as the placid water underneath the surface, giving gratitude for the dead butterflies for lighting the way.

"Honk...Honk...Honk... Honk...Honk...Honk..."

Queer distant sounds grew close. When she turned to see where they were coming from, her heart remained calm no more but boomed like an erupted volcano. A flock of thousands of geese were whizzing down from the north; their noise was deafening. Grey wings covered the blue sky, and their long black necks appeared like a cloud of arrows, threatening to spear her from behind.

Grace beat her wings in panic and dived to avoid the deadly swarm, but she was too late. Goose feathers slapped her from left and right until her eyes darkened. A moment later, she turned into a sailplane without a wind, sinking toward the glimmering water.

The lake surface appeared blurry and the honks faded. Grace fell into a glowing bright light. "Now I am dead," she said, and glanced up at her radiant brothers in the sky, ready to become one.

Hours later she opened her eyes. Nothing but blue water surrounded her, yet her wings remained dry.

"Where am I? Am I dead?"

"Not yet, monarch, but almost..." a voice spoke.

Grace glanced to her left and stared at a bright white lotus.

"You are quite fortunate," said the lotus. "I watched you falling all the way down beside me."

Grace said nothing. She lay on a floating reed basket next to the stunning lotus. Grey powder filled the inside of the drifting box.

"What are you doing here all by yourself, lotus?" Grace asked.

"We are never alone, butterfly, but surrounded by life. Just open your eyes."

Grace shifted her human sight into the monarch's vision. Birds were flying, fish swam in the lake, and the sun played hide and seek with a few scattered clouds. The flower spoke the truth. Life existed everywhere, and the mind that sees clearly never feels lonely.

"What is this container?" Grace asked

"It is a floating grave," said the lotus in a calm voice.

"A grave?" Grace repeated in disbelief.

"A family planted me in their home pond. Then, they scattered the ashes of their beloved one into the water. When I bloomed from the murky water, they released me to the vast lake in her memory. She had a lovely spirit indeed," said the flower.

Grace glanced at the lotus; her straw-like mouth unfurled in astonishment.

"You seemed surprised..." the lotus smiled.

"I am," said the monarch. "You don't sing or dance, nor do you speak like the other wildflowers. Instead, peace and radiance spread from your lovely petals."

"Well... perhaps I am different. Some say the lotus is the butterfly of the flowers."

"Butterfly?" she exclaimed, not expecting to hear such an answer.

"We are the masters of transformation among our brother and sister flowers. The same as you are among the bugs. Under the dirty water we grow, seeing no light or hope, only filth and darkness. When our slimy stems are tired of the dirt and question their purpose, he comes."

"Are you speaking of the wizard of light?"

"That's right, butterfly. His visit encourages us to become what we can be. He tells us the light is slightly above our heads and the murky water. Those of us who choose to believe him continue to push our way through and emerge from the water as heavenly lotuses. Others, who are confused and in utter doubt, drop down and die in the mud. Those poor ones live an empty life, never fulfilling their purpose."

Grace's heart saddened. She had learned that many caterpillars died in their chrysalis from panic and fear. They didn't believe they could change and refused to accept the transformation.

Suddenly, the faces of people she knew came into her mind,

including herself. Blind to the light and love life had to offer, they had decided instead to dig their heads into the dirt, living in fear and anger and guilt—far, far from their potential.

"I thought only butterflies transformed...I guess I was wrong," said Grace after a long silence.

"Life contains the seed of growth and change," said the lotus. "Because of that, anything alive can adapt and grow. Yet, transformation is first and foremost a decision, a free choice that has been given to all living things. You know I speak the truth, for if not you wouldn't have transformed from a caterpillar into a monarch."

Grace moved restlessly in her spot. "Actually, I only observed it but didn't go through a transformation myself. I hope to achieve it during my journey."

Now, it was the lotus's turn to be stunned, and so Grace shared her story with the lovely flower.

"Incredible!" said the lotus. "You are a daughter of light in a monarch body. I am blessed indeed to witness such a thing."

All of a sudden, the floating basket bumped into something. Grace's heart bounced, and she leaped into the air.

"I am on the other side of the lake. I survived," she screamed, laughing and looping around with joy. The lake's bank had gray rocks and shrubs, nothing familiar. She landed on the lotus with her happy feet. "Thank you for your wisdom, kingly flower. I will share your lessons with others on my journey south."

The lotus swayed and opened some more, sensing the sun. "My petals are telling me we are on the northern bank," said the flower.

Grace's heart froze. "No, no, it can't be," she muttered and glanced at the sun. The ball of fire was indeed climbing down to her left. Her wings crumpled like an old newspaper, and despair sucked all the remaining nectar from her stomach.

A few hundred yards to the west, she recognized the red maple tree in which she'd nested.

"Argh..." she screamed in frustration.

"Daughter of light," said the lotus in a calm voice, "when I bloomed over the murky water, I watched my brothers underneath the surface. Two had their stems not a fingernail from the light. The first pushed forward and emerged, but the second gave up and died. Don't quit, monarch, no matter what. Your journey is much more significant than you imagine."

Grace said nothing for long moments. Soon, the fog of frustration cleared and calmness took over. *The lotus speaks wisdom*, she thought. All her life, the best things happened to her right after a difficulty that challenged her resolve. Yet, she had never quit and so reaped the rewards.

"I should celebrate that I'm still alive after the deadly accident with the geese," the monarch said at last. She gave a soft kiss to the lotus and flew back to the starting line on the red maple. As she flew over the flowers on the bank, they sang her an encouraging song about the strength and determination of the butterfly.

"They transformed and so will I," decided Grace as she landed on a tall branch.

The red sunset turned the lake into a scarlet mirror. She closed her eyes and reflected on the wisdom of the day, giving gratitude for her experience on the journey. A monarch doesn't count failures, for he doesn't consider them as such. These are all attempts and experiences. As long as one remains on his path, he never fails.

This last thought eased her mind, and she fell asleep early again, waiting for another attempt tomorrow.

The next morning, after dining in the bank's flower restaurant and joining their live orchestra, she flew to the floating basket and landed on the lotus's heart.

"Good morning, daughter of light," called the lotus in a cheerful voice.

"From today, I am Grace the monarch and nothing else," she said.

The lotus cooed, "So be it, monarch. Now, come and feast on me, before you continue your journey."

And so she did, and his nectar was the most delicious of them all.

Moments later she began to travel south again. Long hours she glided and soared and flapped her wings. Flap, flap, flap, glide. Early daybreak grew into late morning, which turned to midday and afternoon. Yet the tenacious monarch kept flying.

Her stomach shrank. When just a bit was left, she spotted the lake's southern bank.

Grace recalled a time her car's fuel level went under the red line when there was no gas station around. Each moment had seemed like an eternity. Now, she felt the same anxiousness, only a hundred times more. She was flying on the last fumes of her nectar, yet the shore looked blurry and didn't seem any closer.

"Please, I need some help," she prayed with all of her little heart.

She could flap no more. The color was beginning to drain away from her brilliant wings and her sight turned gray. The wind kept her floating but only for a little while. At last she began to sink toward the blue water. There was no basket below to save her from the inevitable crash and drowning.

"I am coming, lake." Her tiny tears dropped and formed a sad ripple, one that would carry the news of her death to the flowers on the bank.

Now only twenty feet above the surface, and before Grace closed her eyes forever, she noticed three butterfly shadows on the water. I must be dreaming, she thought.

"Keep your wings straight," a voice commanded from overhead.

Suddenly, from her left and right two monarchs flew along-side her. Each placed one of his wings under her wing while flapping the other. And so the three butterflies flew as one until, minutes later, they crashed on the southern bank with nothing in their tanks.

"You are my guardian angels..." Grace whispered in a faint voice.

"We are more than that," one panted for air. "We are your brothers."

The voice sounded familiar. Grace's eyes opened wide. "Luxrider...!" she mumbled in disbelief and then fainted from exhaustion.

The monarch gazed at her, stunned. He didn't understand how this butterfly knew his name.

CHAPTER 11

"How do you know my name?" Luxrider asked the new member of the band when she opened her eyes again.

"I'm a psychic," Grace chuckled at the two stunned faces, realizing he didn't recognize her as a butterfly. "I heard your friend calling you," she lied.

"Strange," said Luxrider. "I almost feel like we have met before. But it can't be. The only monarch I ran into is my new brother here, Monasero."

At once, the other butterfly jumped to his feet, swirled and bowed. "A pleasure to meet you, my lady," he said with a seductive tone.

Grace and Luxrider exchanged a glance and roared with laughter.

Monasero gave a surprised expression and slapped Luxrider's antennae. "What? Did I do something wrong? Are you laughing at my new dance moves?" he whispered to his friend, hoping the female in the company wouldn't catch his words.

But she did.

"Your dance steps are perfect, brother!" Luxrider teased.

Monasero made Grace think of a Latin lover, what with his dramatic gestures and dances and whispers. Every time he spoke she needed to restrain herself from bursting into laughter.

"Laugh as much as you want, both of you. But at journey's end, the ladies won't be able to resist my smooth dancing."

"I am sure they won't," Grace winked at Luxrider.

"You still didn't tell us your name," said Luxrider to Grace.

She decided to keep the joke as long as she could. "Gaby," she said, which was the first name that came into her head. "Pleasure to meet you, my lords," she imitated Monasero with a soft voice.

They all laughed at once, including the smooth dancer, who was usually the butt of most jokes. The bond between the three of them was instant.

Sunset approached and the three monarchs feasted on the flowers around them, filling their empty stomachs. Next, they found a pine tree and perched on a branch.

Grace sank into her evening meditation, and so did the others. She gazed at the pinkish lake behind her with pride and gratitude. Proud of herself for not giving up and grateful to her courageous new friends whose kindness and compassion saved her from certain death.

Soon, the three shared stories and wisdom from the first part of their journey. When the males heard about the lotus and the flowers on the bank, their tongues unrolled with astonishment. This lady monarch seemed quite special, they thought.

"Time to sleep now," said Luxrider. "Tomorrow, another day is waiting."

Moments later, the two were already snoring.

Grace's exhausted body demanded rest, yet her eyes wandered to her new friends instead. Gazing at Luxrider's wings, a fluttering sensation grew in her stomach. Without thinking, she moved closer and his sweet fragrance dazzled her. A strange craving for his touch made her body tingle and she felt like an excited teenage girl.

Suddenly, the pine needles rustled. She hopped back to her spot.

"I am proud of you, Grace," whispered the wind. "And don't you worry; your secret name is safe with me."

Grace smiled, and minutes later she rejoined her friends.

Dawn rose, and the three musketeers stood ready on the treetop, fighting each other for each ray of the sun.

"There is enough for everyone," laughed the wind. "My older sister is quite generous."

"Congratulations to you all for passing a challenging test," the sun joined the conversation.

They all bowed and thanked her.

"You should thank my younger sister for, without her last gust, none of you would now be standing on the southern shore of the lake."

The wind turned quiet while the monarchs praised her for her loving support. Very rarely did the older sister pay a compliment to the younger, so when it occurred, the wind cherished the moment.

"All right, that's enough!" The sun glowed bright, a bit jealous of her sister's attention. "Now, before you all continue your adventure, share with me some of the things you have learned thus far," said the sun. "Luxrider?"

"I learned everything in life has a purpose, even death. Our glowing monarch brothers that died on their journey showed me the way. Their light and love encouraged me in my most difficult moments."

"Amen to that," cheered the sun. "Monasero?"

"I realized our joy is contagious. Anytime we passed near people their faces beamed at us. Our presence turned their hidden sparkle into a flame, and their light shined, if just for a moment."

"A wisdom teaching indeed," sighed the sun in pleasure. "People of light glow when they gaze upon you because they recognize the butterfly within themselves. The carefree flying beauty they see touches their hearts and minds at the deepest level and beyond their walls of defense. Only love can do that. The more you grow in wisdom and joy, the stronger your light will be—such is the butterfly effect."

The sun glowed on Grace now. "Gr..." A sudden blast cut the sun short. "Gaby?" said the wind, then whispered their secret to her sister sun.

Grace had learned so much in such a brief time that her mind overflowed with knowledge and ideas. She wanted to talk about the teachings of the lake and the flowers and the lotus, yet said nothing of these. Instead, she said, "I learned there is nothing more loving and gracious than caring for a stranger. My two friends here put their lives on the line and took a deadly risk for someone they didn't know. For me. That is why both of them shine with the most beautiful light."

Grace bowed to the two, who changed colors and smiled. The sisters had no words.

A sudden flash glowed between the branches.

It's not the sun, thought Grace. The warmth spread and wrapped around their wings like a soft blanket.

"True love is seeing a stranger as yourself," the wizard of light joined the conversation. "It is a vision beyond forms and appearances. One that unfolds the truth."

"The truth," repeated Grace unwittingly.

"Underneath our separate images, we are all light and

connected to each other as one. And so, when you save a stranger you save yourself, and when you love another, you love yourself."

"But how do we..." mumbled Grace.

But the wizard vanished with a flash.

"The three of you are fortunate indeed," said the sun moments later. "He seldom speaks this sort of wisdom in such an early phase of the journey. Your brilliant realization invoked him to appear, Gaby. Cherish this truth close to your hearts, monarchs."

"Thank you, wise sisters!" called the butterflies as they flew from the tree.

"Quite a band, don't you agree, sister?" The sun laughed, and the wind joined her.

The three musketeers feasted on the abundant daisies and then headed southwest. For the next two days, Captain Luxrider navigated them skillfully through plains and woods, passing towns and farms on their way.

Grace didn't expose her true identity yet; she was waiting for the right moment. Nonetheless, the two became suspicious of her for, as the journey took them further toward their goal, she seemed to perceive much of the world as though it wasn't the first time she had noticed such things. Soon enough, she needed to guard her tongue.

One evening, they perched on an orange tree in the backyard

of a home in a small town. Music began to play as people gathered outside. Soon, their cheers and laughter grew and so did the dancing.

Luxrider and Monasero stared at Grace in disbelief as her feet and head moved to the beat.

"What are you doing?" Monasero gaped at her with an open mouth.

Grace froze as she met their questioning eyes. "Nothing..." she yawned, trying to appear casual, "just stretching."

Monasero shook his head, and a sneaky smile curled his face. "No, no, no Gaby, you can't fool me this time. You were dancing—or at least trying to."

At once, Monasero roared and Luxrider gave a grin while Grace blushed orange.

"No need to be ashamed, Gaby. Monasero is here to teach you!!" he announced. Her threatening glare didn't deter him and in a swift motion he embraced her with his wings and antennae.

For long hours, they swirled and bounced while Monasero showed her all kinds of techniques. At last, she sank on the branch, breathless.

"I hate to admit it, Monasero, but you are a rare talent," she smiled.

The fabulous dancer whirled with laughter and then went to sleep.

Grace caught a look from Luxrider, and she could almost swear it contained a spark of jealousy. Strangely enough, she found herself quite pleased with this discovery. She closed her eyes, but a gentle touch caressed her wings.

"May I, Lady Gaby?" Luxrider touched her with his antenna, and she returned the touch. He embraced her with his left wing and drew her tightly to him.

Grace's heart raced madly, and each breath turned into a gasp. She prayed he wouldn't notice her excitement, but the shiver of her antennae and the orange glow on her face gave her away. Like a precious flower, under his burning gaze she melted into nectar, craving to fulfill his thirst. They danced for minutes only, yet on a timeless dance floor, melting into each other's eyes and hearts.

At last, they separated from each other's wings and retired in silence. Neither of them, however, managed to quiet their minds. They relived their exceptional dance in their dreams over and over until dawn rose.

It was late morning as the three flew over green farm fields. The fragrance of flower hedges along dirt roads pulled them like metal to magnets.

"Look!!" Grace pointed with her antennae. Many orange wings feasted on the white flowers beneath. They rushed down with excitement, ready to imbibe the delicious nectar and meet their new brothers.

"Nnneeaoooowwwwwww..."

A deafening sound passed below them. It was a giant yellow flying butterfly, or at least that was what the boys imagined, racing behind it with cheers.

"Stop!!!! Luxrider! Monasero! Stop!" Grace screamed with all her might, but the noise from the airplane's engine was too loud.

Grace flapped her wings like a frantic hummingbird until she reached her friends.

"Stop!!" she cried beside them, and they halted in the midair.

"What is it, Gaby?" Luxrider asked with a puzzled voice.

Grace said nothing but her concerned eyes followed the yellow airplane. "Just a bad feeling..." she mumbled.

"Girls!" Monasero teased her.

But when they looked ahead none of them smiled. A white mist sprayed from the airplane like poison from a snake's mouth, dropping on the fields below. Moments later, it flew away and vanished into the horizon. What came after, however, became engraved in the minds of the three forever: A glowing monarch soared from the sprayed fields until he froze forever in the midair. Soon enough, more followed, rising like little angels. That first single light turned into a golden path. Not a few but a flock; more than two hundred dead, Grace counted as she shivered beside her friends.

Minutes later, they left the field of death and flew in silence until they stopped at a distant farm. Noon approached, and they drank some nectar but found it rather bitter. It would take time before sweet juice could comfort their broken hearts.

The three monarchs continued southwest for long hours, landing on a pink dogwood tree. It was one of many growing along a white picket fence.

Grace delighted to rest in such beauty and prepared herself for a sunset reflection. But when she turned around, her heart shuddered. Tens of gray stones covered the grassy ground in front of her tree. She was in a cemetery.

"Of all the places you had to choose this one?" her irritated voice snapped at Luxrider. She had seen enough death for to-day.

The two boys exchanged strange glances.

"You don't understand, Gaby," Monasero flitted beside her. "There are free meals here. People of light bring all sorts of flowers and leave them on the gray stones."

Grace stared at him in disbelief. The sight of hundreds of dead monarchs still haunted her, and she cursed the pilot for what he did. And now, seeing her two friends already laughing after the horror of today annoyed her greatly.

"Come, Gaby, let's eat," said Luxrider.

"I am not hungry," she lashed her wings and flew to another

tree, facing away from them.

The two monarchs said nothing. They flew into the field of gray stones, feasting on heavenly nectar from the bunches of flowers. When they returned to their tree, Grace darted blaming glances at them. And so, they remained on their own branch, avoiding the intense anger of their friend.

Sunset passed, and dusk approached yet Grace had difficulty giving gratitude for the cursed day. She swayed restlessly on a twig. A soft breeze kissed the dogwood flowers and Grace sensed the wind's presence.

"What?" she grumbled.

"Calm down, monarch!" the wind spoke with a firm voice. "I am not your enemy, neither are your brothers on the other tree. It is your attitude and your mind that beset you."

Grace breathed, and her nagging voice faded away. "I am sorry...it's just the death of the poor monarchs shook me."

"Death does it to many," said the wind.

"It doesn't seem to affect them much," Grace said, glaring at her companions, her sarcastic tone reawakened.

"Perhaps you should open your eyes then. Instead of blaming your friends for not mourning or grieving the dead and for being so self-righteous, watch them and learn. They are the monarchs of fall. They celebrate life and accept all that comes their way, including death. Grief can't linger too long in the monarch's mind, for he is the king of the present, not king of the past."

"I don't understand..." mumbled Grace. "All my life I feared death and learned how to avoid it. And now you disregard death as though it's just another step on a journey."

"That's right," said the wind. "However, you won't see it as I or the monarchs do unless you open your butterfly's eyes and leave the limited perception of people behind you. How do you view yourself now?"

"I am an orange and black butterfly with four wings and..." Grace described her appearance, but the wind cut her short.

"A true monarch perceives himself as a golden light. He is aware of his antennae and wings, but the light is his essence. And so when the orange wings are eaten by a spider or poison kills the butterfly, he always keeps sight of the eternal. On who he is underneath the orange butterfly: a pure light, which death cannot touch."

Grace stood silent, yet her mind quivered from the wind's wisdom.

"Look at me..." she muttered with despair. "Thinking I am the smart one, expecting and demanding from my friends to see the world as I do. I try to change them so I won't need to, yet they have already transformed. I am the one who needs to grow."

"Don't be harsh on yourself, my child," said the wind with love. "You were doing pretty well until now. Soon, your monarch eyes will open wide, and you shall experience the truth."

"Thank you for your infinite patience, wind. Your grace is like no other."

"Patience is love and I am love, the same as you. Good night, butterfly," whispered the wind and left.

The stars glinted through the dogwood branches. Neither anger nor blame remained in her heart. The wind's counsel had drained that poison from her. With a quiet mind, she gave her gratitude for the day.

Grace gave thanks that the three survived the deadly incident. She thanked the flowers for their nectar and the tasty water of the streams; she thanked the sun and the wind and the trees. A moment later, she flew back to her friends' tree, promising herself not to judge them again.

CHAPTER 12

Luxrider was the first to awaken. The dogwood tree had become moist and wet as drizzle dropped from the cloudy sky.

"Let's find a better cover," he said to his friends.

Moments later, they flew into the heart of the cemetery, where a giant maple stood on a mound.

Monasero gazed at the thick gray clouds. Not a glimpse of sunlight penetrated them. "Rain is coming..."

Soon, the morning grew older but not bright, and the sprinkle became a shower. The three friends embraced each other under the roof of a branch. Grace stared at the rain, annoyed. It was a barrier, hindering her from moving forward on the journey.

"When will it end?" She glared at the clouded sky.

"When it stops raining," answered Monasero with idle eyes and Luxrider smiled.

Nothing seems to disturb these two, she thought. The wisdom of the wind from last night echoed in her head. I am here to observe and learn to become a monarch, she reminded herself. Soon, she forgot about the gloomy weather and joked with her friends. In the afternoon, her empty stomach rumbled like an airplane and the boys almost dropped to the ground from laughing so hard.

"Didn't I tell you yesterday that you should feast on the people's flowers?" Monasero teased her.

She gave him a nasty glare.

"Don't worry, Gaby, the first rain break we will fly out to eat," Luxrider encouraged her. She nodded with a smile.

Suddenly, the sound of cars came from the road. A group of people dressed in black and carrying umbrellas headed uphill toward one of the graves.

"A funeral service..." whispered Grace, eyeing the gathering.

Soon, the people packed around a casket and a man called out a prayer.

"Come, Gaby, the rain stopped!" Monasero's voice shook her from the scene.

"We might have a few minutes before it begins to drop again," said Luxrider.

The two flew away.

"I am coming..." mumbled Grace. But instead of following

her friends, she flapped her wings straight into the crowd.

A man in his late thirties stood beside the coffin. His face was frozen and his eyes were swollen from tears. On his left, a young girl with curly blonde hair and blue eyes gaped at the wet ground. Some women whimpered and men shed tears as an old priest read something out loud.

Grace felt compelled to reach closer to the girl. At once, she flew and landed on the colorful flowers above the coffin. Despite her starving stomach and the luring scent, she didn't touch any. Her eyes remained fixed on the girl. She reminded her of someone from the past: herself.

"Why, Daddy? Why did Mommy leave us?" the little girl asked the man with tears. He kneeled on the muddy ground and kissed his daughter's head softly. "Sweetheart, Mommy is still with us, here, in our hearts," the man pointed at her chest. Yet, she didn't seem to believe her father's words.

All of a sudden, a sparkle of light shined on the casket beside Grace. A sad feminine voice spoke from the light. "I wish I could tell them that I love them one more time," the voice from the light said. "I wish I could tell them I am fine."

Grace gazed at the light and her wings shivered. Without a thought, she flew to the girl, landed on her little palm and wrapped her antennae around the girl's finger. The girl's mouth opened in astonishment.

"Your mother loves you and your daddy very much, little

one," said Grace. "There is nothing to fear. She is alright."

The man looked at his daughter's hand just as the monarch rushed back to the casket flowers.

"Did you see that, Daddy? Did you hear it? Mommy said she loves us, and everything is okay." Her young face turned joyous and bright.

The man nodded, lifted his girl and hugged her tight. His sorrow had been drained from his gloomy cheeks and wonder fell on his eyes as he stared at the monarch.

A puff of wind blew, and the cloaking gray clouds made space for sunlight. Moments later, a heavenly rainbow painted the sky.

"Good job," the sun complemented her sister.

"Thank you from the bottom of my heart, butterfly," said the glowing voice. "You brought my family some peace. You are a true miracle."

Then the mother's light vanished through the crack in the clouds and joined the sun.

Soon the funeral ended, and the little girl threw the monarch a last kiss before she left.

Drops fell again, and Grace's stomach howled like a starving wolf. She leaped on the flowers and sucked nectar furiously before the rain started again. She returned to the tree at the last moment.

"Well, what do you think of the graveyard flowers?"

Monasero's voice welcomed her.

"They are particularly tasty," smiled Grace. A new light and an expression of peace shone from her face for she had just performed a miracle, an act of love. "What were the two of you doing all this time?" she asked the boys.

Luxrider remained silent and seemed quite distant.

"We created miracles, of course," said Monasero.

His answer caught her by surprise as she had expected to hear all about flower nectar and nothing more. "Miracles?" Her eyes grew wide.

"Some people came to visit the gray stones on the other side of the hill," said Monasero.

Grace swallowed. "So what exactly did you do?" she asked offhandedly.

"We floated around them and sang songs."

"That's it? Do you call that a miracle?" Grace shook her head.

Monasero gave her a long, queer stare. "We brought our light near them and soon they glinted like the stars. Their sorrow and sadness dissipated like a fine mist, for darkness doesn't dwell with light. If that isn't a miracle than what is?"

Grace stood silent for a while. "I thought to perform a miracle you need to do something extraordinary," she mumbled.

"Remember the teachings," Luxrider joined the conversation. "In the right state of mind, a monarch's presence is a miracle. Being the kings of the present moment and seeing ourselves as the light casts away the darkness around us. When our light glows, the people shine with us. None can be exposed to the light yet remain in the dark."

Grace listened and said nothing. Later, each one fell into a deep stillness and gave thanks for the day and his lessons.

The half moon glowed when Grace opened her eyes. Monasero snored beside her, but Luxrider wasn't there. She scanned the tree for long moments. A silhouette of a butterfly appeared on the far edge of a branch, staring at the sky. Grace shoved Monasero, who seemed to be in the middle of a sweet dream.

"What?" he growled.

"Ssh..." she pointed ahead. "What is wrong with Luxrider?"

"Nothing, don't worry about him. He needs some time alone, that's all," said Monasero, and closed his eyes.

"Don't you lie to me. He is troubled. What happened?" Grace persisted.

"I can't tell you... It's a secret..." he tried to avoid her stern gaze, but nothing helped.

"You better talk or I won't let you sleep tonight," she hissed.

"All right, all right..." snapped Monasero. After a long silence, he spoke again.

"Today we saw a lady sobbing by herself on one of the graves. Her grief and pain cloaked her like a dark shadow. No matter how much we swirled and danced and sang, the light in her remained hidden. Darkness ruled her mind."

Grace's heart froze like ice as she recalled herself weeping at her father's grave.

"After long minutes, Luxrider seemed frustrated and left," continued Monasero. "'It's no use,' he said to me later. When I asked him why, he told me about one particular daughter of light who had saved his life from a spider's web. Her light gleamed brighter than gold, yet she couldn't see it in herself, he said. 'I shared with her my transformation and the wizard's wisdom, but she was afraid to change,' he told me. 'When I convinced the wizard to let her join the monarchs' journey so that she might learn and transform, she still refused. I was naive to believe her to be different,' he told me at last."

Grace turned silent yet her tiny heart stirred like a raging sea. Luxrider's harsh words pierced her wounded pride without mercy. However, the more she pondered it, the more she realized he had said nothing but the truth. That was the way she had lived her life as a person.

Monasero gazed at his friend's silhouette and lowered his eyes. "Luxrider gave that lady his butterfly kiss. There will be no mating for him."

"What are you talking about, Monasero?" Grace's voice trembled.

"When monarchs kiss, it is a bond for life. Luxrider gave up the chance of finding his soul mate by kissing the daughter of light. Her transformation seemed more important to him at the time."

Grace shivered on the branch. No words could express the mixed feelings that swirled in her heart. Love and anger, guilt and annoyance tangled with joy and admiration. At once, she left Monasero behind and flew to the silhouette, landing beside him.

"Is that true, what you told Monasero today? Did you kiss the daughter of light so she might transform into a monarch?"

Luxrider kept gazing at the moon, then he nodded. "I don't understand," mumbled Grace in disbelief. "You fly thousands of miles so you can learn from the wizard about true love, yet you gave up your chance to experience it. What is the purpose of your journey then?" Her moist eyes were full of blame.

"She needed it more than me," answered Luxrider genuinely. "When I noticed her doubts and fears, sadness and anger, and the tremendous agony with which she lived her life, I wanted to help. She was glowing with light yet her own mind kept her in darkness. I only wished her to experience what I went through, the gift of transformation. Perhaps I gave up my opportunity to find my soul mate, but I never gave up on true love. Seeing the other as she truly is, underneath her shape and form, is the truth, and accepting her as the light and nothing else is love."

Grace gazed at Luxrider; her heart almost stopped. Beyond

his attractive wings and alluring scent, a light glowed like no other. Her antennae vibrated with a joy and excitement she had never sensed before. At that moment, each cell in her body and every speck of her golden light knew she was looking at her soul mate. She wrapped him in her wings and gave him her first butterfly kiss.

"I am your Grace, Luxrider," she whispered with joyous tears. "I am the daughter of light."

CHAPTER 13

Golden dawn rose on a clear blue sky, and the two new lovers still lingered in each other's wings.

Monasero rubbed his eyes in disbelief while his straw mouth rolled and unrolled like a yo-yo. "What is this..." he mumbled finally.

Moments later, Luxrider and Grace told him about her real identity and unbelievable story.

"So you are the daughter of light! Remarkable!! I knew you were different from us..." Monasero shook his head. "That explains why you remained immune to my charm."

And so the three musketeers flew for long days toward the southwest. The two sisters visited from time to time and nourished them with more wisdom.

Grace's heart was radiating constant light; her body couldn't contain the love and peacefulness she felt. Now she wasn't just a butterfly but a monarch in love. Lighter than the wind and freer than an eagle. Her grace grew like a blossoming flower, spreading royal fragrance between earth and sky.

Minutes and hours united into the ocean of now, where time had no meaning. Soon, she found no reason to rush to her journey's end. Instead, Grace cherished the present along with her lover and with her good friend.

Every day brought excitement and spectacular scenery. They passed by the bluegrass plains of Kentucky and endless ranches with droves of horses below their wings. Streams wound through the green land like silver hairs, leading them to the fields of Tennessee. Soon enough, hills and mountains clothed in red, orange, and yellow trees appeared. It seemed as though autumn was flying ahead of them, painting the ground with sunset colors.

One afternoon, as the three glided above the plains, they stopped in midair.

"What happened here?" Luxrider mumbled in disbelief.

Logs and bushes were spread out on the barren soil, all dead and dry. The stunned band sailed south for long miles surrounded by the death scene.

"Why?" asked Monasero with a sad note. "Look at the destroyed milkweed everywhere. Our beloved mothers laid our eggs on these plants so we, as caterpillars, could eat the leaves once we'd hatched, and then transform into monarchs. Without the milkweed, the monarchs are doomed. Our existence depends on this plant."

His words stabbed Grace's heart. Huge yellow tractors and trucks were driving down below, and the soil of mother earth turned to powder under their mighty wheels. Miles of milkweed plants had been ruined, and the fog of uncertainty clouded some of the monarchs' future.

"Welcome to the city of Bellamord. Tomorrow is here!" said a gigantic green sign with a picture of smiling people.

A cursed future, built on the destruction of other living things, Grace blazed from within. More than anything, she was ashamed of the ignorance of her brothers and sisters. Not people of light, but people of darkness, she thought. They bring death into the liveliness of the earth.

Hours later they found unspoiled land and feasted on some nectar. Yet none of these flowers sang. They stood as silent as the grave and seemed to share the sadness of their three guests. A gust of wind carried the sounds of the monster machines, and the scent of death spread out. The three lost their appetite and flew far away toward the south.

On an oak tree, they perched and gazed to the west. Majestic purple clouds and a pink horizon set their minds to a sunset reflection yet didn't boost their hearts.

Grace sensed a tense silence building; even Luxrider's cuddle felt cold and distant.

"Why would the people of light do such a thing?" he spoke

to her from his heart. "We, the monarchs, always lift their spirits and shine so they will discover their own light. Why would they want to hurt us? Why don't they return love with love?"

Grace lowered her eyes and shook her head. "I don't think they do it on purpose. Most of them are just not aware. They don't realize the consequences of their actions." She sighed with frustration.

"Don't they understand we are all connected and depend on each other?" Monasero asked. "The flowers feed the monarchs and we spread their seeds in return. We are the light riders, glowing with love and spreading joy and blessings wherever we fly. Without our presence, the world won't be the same. People of light won't discover the sparkle that ignites their fire."

"You are both right." Grace's voice was filled with shame. "I am sorry...I really am."

"Don't be," said Monasero. "You are here with us for a purpose. At journey's end, you will return to the people and make them aware. You will make a difference."

Grace nodded with a lifeless smile and her eyes lost their sparkle. She darted a glance at Luxrider, who also wore a frozen expression on his face. Monasero's words made them realize that though they had found each other in a miraculous way, it was only to be separated at the finish line. This painful thought shattered Grace's heart and a painful burn flamed in her body. "It's not fair..." she muttered at last.

Luxrider embraced her. "Your purpose and journey are above all. You will share with your people a priceless gift, much more precious than anything else."

"I never felt like this before." Tears dropped from her eyes. "Many times I believed I was in love, but now I understand the difference. Why should I give up my heart?"

"You won't, my Grace. True love is never lost; it becomes part of who you are, your essence and light. Wherever you go and whatever you do, it will be part of you, and so will I."

Grace breathed again and squeezed her soul mate tightly. His wisdom warmed her as much as his wings.

In the morning, the musketeers flew again, but they stopped half an hour later.

"Luxrider! Monasero! Come, you must see this," Grace called with excitement and they followed her.

Soon, they all landed on a pine tree near a chainlink fence. There they beheld hundreds of children raking and digging the soil while others carried black pots in their hands.

"What are they doing?" asked Monasero, sensing a familiar scent in the air.

"They are planting milkweed for the monarchs." Grace's eyes glinted on the children with pride.

A large sign with an orange butterfly painted on it read: "Bring back the monarchs."

"Some of them destroy our habitat while others build and

plant," said Monasero to Luxrider. "They care about us!"

"Indeed!" cheered Luxrider. "Let's pay them a visit of gratitude."

At once, he floated over the school fence and the two followed him, all singing for the young people of light. Grace noticed how they all turned, wearing broad smiles and cheering, excited by the presence of the butterflies.

"You see, children!" called a beaming teacher. "Plant it and they will come..."

Grace laughed and swirled with joy. The little ones restored her trust in humans. There is still much good in people, she thought. They just need to be informed and wake up.

A few more days passed, and the band continued their journey south. They flew over cities and towns and farms while Grace explained many of the things they saw.

"People of light are quite complex," said Monasero after she described an electrical power plant and its use.

When they crossed the open fields and glided through forests and mountains, her two companions shared their vast knowledge with her. Grace was stunned time and again. Her friends' experienced nature with exceptional depth. They told her about the hearts of the trees and the voices from the ground. At first she had a hard time sensing these but the more she became a butterfly, the more she became one with all.

"Everything is truly connected," she whispered to Luxrider,

placing her antennae on a pine bark.

The tree's ancient heart beat slowly yet steadily. Grace could sense the flow of life through roots to feed stems, limbs, and needles. Now she knew what a pine tree was. Not by learning the facts and labels, but by connecting with his essence and light. The eternal energy beyond form.

"You begin to open your butterfly's eyes, my love," Luxrider stroked her wings.

"The world is magical and filled with light," said Grace with wondering eyes.

As they reached the southern part of Louisiana, a thick mist covered the land. They tried to go around the fog but it spread for long miles, and they hadn't enough time or energy to prolong their flight. Dusk approached, and the monarchs landed on a cypress tree.

"I don't like this place," mumbled Grace.

"We have no choice," answered Luxrider with a tired voice.

Exhausted from the day, they desired to rest. But when darkness fell, none of them dared to shut his eyes. Shrieks, vibrations through the branches, and constant chirps went on for hours. Deadly hunters surrounded them, and no musketeers' swords could make them safe.

A new day rose yet brought no comfort to the monarchs. The fine mist dissipated only to reveal a giant swamp. Murky green water spread throughout the area and covered much of the trees trunks under the water.

"We are trapped..." Monasero muttered.

The marsh seemed to enclose them from every direction. No wind blew, and the air turned humid and suffocating. An alligator peeked from the surface, sneaking up behind a great blue heron. On their left, a praying mantis squashed a bug and dragonflies were butchering any insects that dared fly.

"This is a graveyard. It stinks of death." Grace shuddered on the branch.

"We will find a way through," said Luxrider with a calm voice, but his gaze seemed far from certain.

The morning turned to noon, but the sun barely penetrated the canopy of trees. None of them moved. They froze in utter silence at their spot.

"We can't stay here forever," said Monasero. "I am the best flier of all of us. I will fly first and draw any attention to me. You two should stay far behind me."

"It's too dangerous, brother," said Luxrider.

"Do you have another idea?" Monasero asked. No one spoke. "That's what I thought. No worries. Let me show these dragonflies who is the greatest dancer in the swamp."

Luxrider and Grace nodded with a smile. Monasero hadn't lost his sense of humor, no matter what the situation brought.

"Please be careful, my friend," said Grace.

The three huddled together and prayed for a successful

flight.

A moment later the great dancer soared and left the tree. Grace and Luxrider watched carefully and followed from behind. Not a minute had passed when the sounds of zoom and buzz cut through the humid air. A deadly chase began. Two dragonflies charged Monasero's tail, speeding at him from behind. The monarch diverted to the right, dived near the murky water and raced through the trees' branches. At last, the hunters gave up and searched for easier prey.

Monasero flew with the arrogant air of a peacock, drawing to him most of the predators while his two friends flew almost unnoticed. He escaped hunting birds and spider webs and wasps, dancing and spinning like a Topgun pilot.

Grace and Luxrider cheered for their friend, whose confidence grew sky-high. He was the king of the air, and the sky was his palace dance floor.

An hour later, grassy fields came into sight. Their hearts lifted to the heavens as the three monarchs regrouped.

"Behold!" Luxrider called. "Monasero, the wind dancer is here!"

"Yeehaw!!" screamed Grace, poking Monasero's wing. "Songs will be sung praising your flight, master of the marsh!" she declared.

The marvelous dancer laughed hard. Seeing his beloved friends alive and well was all that mattered to him. They reached the edge of the murky water, and bright pink lilies welcomed them.

"I am starving for some exquisite nectar," Monasero chuckled and dived toward the colorful flowers. His friends followed him from behind.

"The flowers are not singing..." Grace thought aloud. At once, her wings grew tense.

"Monas..." Grace screamed his name as the dancer landed on a white water lily. Her terrifying scream made Monasero bounce back into the air.

In a split second, a lurking frog beside the flower jumped from the surface like a rocket. Monasero swirled and spun acrobatically, but it was his final dance. The green predator caught him in his giant mouth and tore him apart. Grace's heart dropped to the bottom of the murky swamp, refusing to beat again. Instead of flying away, she froze in midair, vulnerable to other hunters' attacks. Luxrider needed to slap her with his wings until she came out of her shock. Then, together, they flew toward the west and collapsed on the first tree they encountered, a weeping willow.

When the two turned around, all that remained of their beloved brother was a frozen glowing butterfly, stuck above the marsh's edge.

"A paralyzed dancer, never to dance again..." Grace wept, and the willow joined her.

CHAPTER 14

Sunset arrived and the sun painted the heavens with only one color, bloody red. No pink, no purple, no orange. With that the old sister saluted Monasero, the sky dancer.

Luxrider held to a twig and whispered a song for his fallen brother. "We shall meet once again on the dance floor of life, my good friend..."

Grace stood on another branch. Her butterfly's mind deserted her, and the old human mind hurried to clasp the void, seizing her with mighty claws, grief on the left and fear on the right. Monasero, her lively dancing companion, was no more. She missed his jokes and wisdom, his swirls, and funny gestures. The vivid image of his death whipped her body, and the open wounds bled pain.

Luxrider watched her agony in silence, giving her space to experience and reflect in her own way. After all, it was her journey, her transformation. He loved his brother so much, and the sadness filled him also. Nevertheless, he had a monarch mind. A golden one that kept him in the present moment and drained the pain from his heart. Soon enough, he gave thanks for his friend's trusted company and for surviving the swamp with his soul mate.

Later that night, the wizard visited Grace.

"His spirit was strong," he said. "His zealous light will join his brothers and guide many on their way."

The monarch said nothing, yet her eyes blurred with tears.

"You have progressed a great deal in your journey, Grace, and have grown much in wisdom and love. Keep up the good work and hang on to your butterfly's mind."

"He loved to spin and dance," she forced a smile. "Now he is lost."

"His butterfly body is lost but not his essence. Love is an eternal light that changes form, nothing more. I am sure Monasero will continue to dance in another form. A dancer always remains a dancer."

The wizard's words cast grief from Grace's heart, and hope entered in its place. "Love doesn't die...There is nothing to fear..." she repeated to herself as the wizard left.

As sunset had bled red, sunrise shone gold. The sky artist splashed only one color again, this time rustic orange, similar to the monarch's wings.

Luxrider and Grace began their day meditation. A first morning without their brother beside them seemed quiet and strange. Yet life was larger than death and carried them along on their journey. The two drank some nectar and flew southwest. Soon enough, they found themselves roaming through woods of pines and oaks.

"Texas..." gasped Grace, gazing at a gigantic flapping lone star flag. More than twelve hundred miles she had traveled. Not bad for an insect weighing less than a paper clip.

Luxrider led the way through crowded pinewoods until they opened onto a grassy savanna. Oak trees spread throughout this region, and white-tailed deer roamed among them. Soon, barbed wire fences stretched everywhere, and cowboys on horses herded longhorn cattle on the vast land.

On the fourth day since they left the swamps, the two monarchs stopped in a small town.

Gray clouds cloaked the sky, and no warmth or light penetrated the thick blanket.

"A storm is coming," said Luxrider. "We better find a safe shelter."

They filled their stomachs with nectar drawn from some backyard flowers. Minutes later, thunder roared and blue lightning bolts cracked the air. Rain started pouring, and the two found cover under a back patio roof. Smoke climbed out from the brick chimney, and Grace peeped through the glass window at the back.

A couple was lying on the living room sofa, watching TV. The logs in the fireplace glowed red. Grace smiled. One of her favorite things was to sit beside a crackling fire while it was raining outside. The dancing flames and scent of burning wood always eased her mind. Her wings shivered as she craved the cozy warmth again. Luxrider pulled her to him and the heat of his body eased her mind. No fire equaled Luxrider's, she thought, and rubbed his head.

Hours later, the slam of a door shook the patio and woke them. The man paced from side to side, his face red and angry as he smoked a cigarette with a nervous expression. Inside, the woman gazed at the TV with an icy face. Then she jumped to her feet, stormed through the living room and peeped through the back door.

"You are an idiot, Brian! An idiot!" she barked and banged the door behind her, disappearing into the hallway.

The man said nothing but smoked his cigarette like a steaming locomotive, grumbling to himself. Shortly after, he went inside and sank on the couch with a miserable face.

Grace and Luxrider peered through the glass again. Framed pictures of a cheerful wedding and the couple kissing crowded the wood fireplace mantle.

"I don't understand," mumbled Luxrider. "They seemed so happy together. I wonder what went wrong."

"Life...is what went wrong," Grace stared through the window but saw nothing except her own miserable past.

Luxrider gave her a puzzled stare. He didn't grasp her meaning. "But life is not good, nor bad. Life is the force underneath everything," he said.

She turned silent, pondering his words. "I meant situations," she finally said. "Harsh events that occur in life, pulling us down and squashing our expectations. This couple fell in love once, but time has a way of eroding love."

A bright light came beside them, and the two hearts boomed with joy. "Each visit of the wizard is a rare privilege," the sisters had told them more than once.

"Nothing can erode true love, my dear monarchs," said the wizard. "Love is not a rock that water might crack or a mountain the wind and storms can shape. It is the light in all. It might be hidden, yes, yet never diminishes."

"But this couple was once in love," said Grace. "Why do they turn into each other's worst enemy?"

"People's notion of love is quite different than the monarchs'. At first, they feel a desire and attraction to a person. Next, the bond gets stronger, and they start living together. Later, they find faults in each other, and the freshness and lightness of the relationship begin to fade. Criticism and anger step in, and soon enough the beloved partner is blamed for all the misery and unhappiness suffered by the other. You already know where this road leads, Grace, for you have traveled on it yourself," said the wizard.

Grace stood silently, reflecting upon her past miserable relationships, which had turned into a series of horror movies.

Then, the wizard continued. "Miracles and love follow your steps when you are in the right state of mind. If no expectations, demands, and chains to control the other exist, you will experience true love. A lasting love, one you don't blindly fall into, and you don't fall out of."

Earsplitting thunder and blue bolts of lightning followed the wizard's words and lit the darkness. Grace gazed at Luxrider and knew the wizard spoke the truth. She had lived a life where every relationship started as a thrill; then she found herself floating on a cloud of expectations. Yet, each cloud dissipated after a while, especially those built on demands. Seeking someone else to complete her, to make her feel beautiful, happy and smart, doomed each experience at the start.

Now, next to Luxrider, her love radiated from the depths of her soul. She didn't look for him to complete her in any way or form and placed no expectations or demands upon him. Love flowed from her because she accepted herself as a monarch and became one with all.

"To enter the realm of miracles," the wizard cut into her thoughts, "you must take responsibility for your own emotions and happiness. The time has come to seize the golden reins again and capture your miraculous mind. Enjoy the thunder and lightning, monarchs; the clouds are providing quite a show." And with that, the wizard vanished with laughter.

The two bowed and gave gratitude for his blessed visit.

After each conversation with the wizard or with the two sisters, Grace felt as though a few old chains of her human mind broke. Ideas and concepts she grew up with and believed all her life melted into the wisdom of light. Her mind became looser and freer, fresh, like fruitful spring soil, ready to absorb seeds of truth and grow blossoms.

She glanced through the window. The man still wore a sour face. Compassion filled her heart for the unnecessary pain and agony people live their lives with. *If I make it to the end*, Grace thought...but stopped at once. Any time she heard herself voicing doubt, fear or any negative statement, she halted and re-phrased her voice. *When I reach my journey's end*, she now thought, *I will make a difference. I will show my brothers and sisters the joy of the monarchs*, she promised herself, and her spirit flowed with purpose.

A sudden light came from another window at the back wall. Luxrider went back to sleep, but Grace flew toward it, still under the patio cover.

A young girl about twelve years old sat on a chair and painted on a standing whiteboard. Brushes, pencils, and many paint colors were loaded on the desktop beside her. Grace watched, mesmerized. The girl with the brunette hair was drawing and painting with a dreamy smile on her face. She appeared fully present while creating, and delight spilled from her glinting eyes.

At once, the monarch left the window and returned to her spot. Her tiny heart ached with every breath she drew and tears of the past dropped down. Years ago, Grace stood just as that girl did. Painting was her first love, passion, and joy. Yet, she abandoned it for a vocation of prestige and financial security. The rat race of society dragged her in and she sold her artist's soul to become a lawyer. Soon after, the rainbow colors in her life left her for the gray and black. Her wild, vibrant spirit had been tamed by others' will, and the butterfly within her flew no more.

At that moment, Grace decided to revive her wings and be true to herself instead of to others.

CHAPTER 15

The next day the pouring rain came down even harder. About noon, the lady went out to the patio, a phone in her hand. A low, somber voice came from the speaker.

"Amy...your husband was in a severe car accident. He is in a coma now," said a woman's voice.

The wife's hand shook, almost dropping the phone. "Brian..." her lips shuddered in disbelief. Tears gushed from her terrified eyes, and she fell to her knees. "Where is he?" asked the weeping wife, trying to control her trembling voice.

"He is in the local hospital; you should come at once. The doctors say he might not last the night. I am sorry, dear...I really am," said the voice and hung up.

"Please God...please...don't take him away... I am sorry for everything I said. I beg you..." she wept and dragged herself into the house.

Luxrider and Grace exchanged shocking glances. The

thunderstorm outside seemed nothing compared to the emotional distress they had witnessed. With a concerned heart, Grace flew to the girl's bedroom window and peeped in.

The mother was sitting on the bed beside her daughter, telling her the dreadful news. At first, the girl's face froze in utter shock. Then, she sobbed into the pillow, and her pain hit Grace like a tsunami. Minutes later, the two left the house, rushed to their blue Ford Taurus and raced into the wet street.

"I wish I could help them," said Grace to her soul mate.

He said nothing but hugged her.

For two more days, the storm continued nonstop—and then, it was over.

No one had returned home during the storm, and Grace guessed that the worst had happened.

Dawn rose and painted the few remaining clouds pink and gold. Anxious to leave the patio and resume their journey, the two monarchs flew to the roof and basked in the sun. Steam ascended from the brown shingles while the two meditated. At last, they feasted on the garden flowers like starving wolves, for they hadn't eaten during the storm.

"Wait," called Grace to Luxrider as he prepared to fly. She fluttered to the girl's window one last time, sending her blessings and courage to confront her loss. But when she touched the windowpane, her unfurled tube stuck to the glass like glue; she couldn't tear herself away. The girl's whiteboard revealed a mesmerizing painting. A majestic carpet of Texas bluebonnet flowers clothed a hill and pinkish sunset clouds scattered in the sky. Between the navy blue blossoms and the light blue heaven floated a brunette girl with a monarch's orange wings.

"She painted herself half human and half monarch..." whispered Grace with tears. "The same as me." She recalled one of the sisters' lessons: "When coincidence happens more than once or twice, know that you must be stepping on a miraculous path. Never stray!"

"Come on! We should move," called Luxrider.

Grace darted a last glance at the painting and joined her soul mate.

The two traveled over buildings and homes throughout the small city. Not many cars were on the roads. Perhaps it's Sunday, she thought. As they flew above a pointy building, she halted in mid-air.

"What is it?" asked Luxrider.

"Listen..." she said as faint singing came from inside. The voices pulled her down like heavenly nectar. But then her eyes wandered onto the pitched roof and fell on the cross. Her curious heart hardened at once.

The only time she ever visited a church in Toronto was when her mother died.

"What is this place?" Luxrider hovered beside her.

"Only a church, a place where people gather and pray,"

Grace explained briefly.

She turned to fly south, but her eyes caught something above the entrance. "Grace Church" was written in bold black letters on an orange sign.

Her heart raced. By now she had learned to listen to her gut and view the world as a monarch does. One thing is for certain, she thought. This banner is an omen.

Without a word, she dived to one of the church's open windows and landed on the sill. A moment later, Luxrider stood on her left.

The old building seemed average in size and contained no more than two hundred people. Rows of wooden seats were set on each side of an aisle decked out in a red carpet. Dim light shined through the tall painted glass windows on both sides of the church. On the platform, a young choir sang gently, and Grace found the resentment in her fading away.

"Their voices shake the heart," whispered Luxrider.

Grace nodded and smiled.

"Why are we here?" he asked her with a calm voice.

"I am not sure," she said. "I just feel that I need to be here."

Moments later, she told him about the butterfly painting and the sign on the church. "They must be omens, Luxrider," she said. "Do you believe me?"

"It doesn't matter what I think. A monarch should always follow his heart," he winked at her.

The choir children ended their song and came off the stage, all except one. A brunette girl remained and whispered into the pastor's ears. He gave a nod and hugged her.

Grace gasped. "It's the girl, Luxrider! There, on the stage!"

He recognized her and chuckled. "A butterfly never questions his intuition."

"My brothers and sisters," called the pastor on the platform, "as we speak, our friend Brian is in the hospital in a coma. Let us pray on behalf of our beloved brother."

Tears trickled down the girl's cheeks as she stepped down and joined her mother in the first row.

Soon enough, the place turned as quiet as a graveyard. Eyes shut and lips moved without a sound.

When Grace glanced beside her, Luxrider was gone. She found herself joining the people and praying for a man she didn't know. She asked for him to be well and return to his family. Visions of Brian waking up and hugging his daughter rushed through her mind. Suddenly, her heart started singing an ancient song, a song with neither words nor tune yet filled with beauty and light. It was a pure expression of love.

At the same moment, Grace touched the depth of her soul and the universe itself. Galaxies and stars were traveling around her, and space and time became obstacles no more. She turned into a golden light in the midst of it all, feeling like the creator himself. Nothing seemed impossible.

She had no idea how long she remained in that magical realm. Minutes? A half an hour? Perhaps a full one? She cared nothing about time and melted into the timelessness instead.

A sudden gust of wind blew the French windows wide open. The sun shone, and the dim church grew bright. People who had been sitting soundlessly until now murmured with wondering eyes.

Grace opened her eyes. She heard a distant song yet, scanning the people, none of them sang or made a sound. Her heart raced like pistons in a Ferrari, pumping words to her mouth.

"The monarchs of fall carry the light

To embrace all with love that is bright

No limit, no fear dwells in our minds

So shall we bring miracles to the blind."

Without a thought, Grace flapped her wings and roamed along the center aisle as though it were a field of flowers. Flap, flap, flap, glide. She chanted her song and danced her dance and cared nothing of the dazed faces that followed her. A pure joy and peace flowed from her heart, and her light turned golden.

The wind grew bold and the sun laughed and glowed, and the congregants remained in utter shock. Nonetheless, their astonishment compared to a grain of sand in a desert storm to what came next.

Swarms of orange gushed through the church windows and zoomed around the stunned faces. Grace froze along with the people.

"Come on, brothers and sisters," called Luxrider above all. "Let's show the people of light how a real choir sings!!"

At once, the thousands of monarchs circled the wooden seats and sang their song:

"The monarchs of fall carry the light

To embrace all with love that is bright

No limit, no fear dwells in our mind

So shall we bring miracles to the blind."

With every spin and word, the people's light radiated more. Some glowed in yellow, others in violet and blue, and soon enough a beautiful rainbow was established in Grace Church.

Grace joined her flying friends and tears of joy trickled down her eyes.

The pastor, who had preached all his life about miracles, witnessed his first one now. He stood on the platform with parted lips and blessed the creator for his wonders.

In the pews, men laughed like boys and ladies wiped tears of happiness.

At last the task of the monarchs was accomplished. They left through the open windows, having awakened each and every heart, reminding them to glow.

Only one monarch remained, and she landed on the girl's palm. The young brunette gazed at Grace with moist eyes. "Thank you, monarch, for answering my prayer," she said.

"You are a miracle like no other."

The girl had just finished her words when the phone jingled in her mother's hand.

"Amy..." a female voice trembled on the other side of the line. "You won't believe it, Amy... Brian is awake. He is fine. The doctors say it's a miracle..." the voice choked.

Amy's swollen eyes beamed at the butterfly on her daughter's hand.

"I believe in miracles," said Amy with glinting eyes.

"Me too, Mommy, me too," the girl hugged her mother.

When the girl turned to look, the monarch wasn't there. She had flown carefree through the window to continue her miraculous journey.

CHAPTER 16

"Luxrider! Luxrider!" Grace called, joining the orange cloud that floated faster than any of the white, puffy clouds higher up.

"I am here, Grace," he answered among the thousands of wings—yet she recognized him at once. A monarch could find his soul mate amidst millions, for their hearts beat as one.

"Did you see the people's faces, Luxrider? Did you see their vivid lights?" She laughed beside him, spinning like an aerobatic plane.

Luxrider laughed and swirled with her. Watching her transformation had made his heart sing. The daughter of light was turning into a graceful monarch.

"How did you find all the monarchs?" she asked without a breath.

"It wasn't me who found them, Grace; it was your prayer," he replied.

Grace stared at him, all puzzled.

He explained. "I like to pray while I am flying," said Luxrider. "So I left the window and floated above the building, sensing the wind and the sun with me. At that moment, an intense beam of light came from the church and reached the sky. Not a minute had passed when an orange cloud approached from the north, singing a song that shook my heart. I rushed to the monarchs and led them inside. It was your prayer, Grace. Your prayer soared like an eagle and touched the soul of the universe. When this happens, no force can deny what you ask."

Grace stopped spinning. Now it was her mind swirling from the meaning of Luxrider's words. Was it possible she possessed such power?

"It must have been the people's prayers," she muttered, refusing to accept the idea that such strength dwelled within her.

"It was you," Luxrider insisted. "The two sisters will be my witnesses. I watched the light of the people's prayers climbing up slowly and then fading away. But yours! It flashed like a fiery column and pierced the sky."

"Why?" Grace asked. "They were many and they knew this man better than I. Why was my prayer answered and not theirs?"

Luxrider remained silent as he pondered her question.

"Well, well, finally someone found the secret of a prayer," roared the wizard, who had taken the form of a golden butterfly and flew between them. "Luxrider spoke the truth, Grace. Many times I have witnessed people's prayers. Their light climbs slowly and uncertainly, like cigarette smoke. Up and up and up, drifted by the wind and dwindling; rarely do they reach the heavens. Their good will and intentions make their light rise, yet their doubts and lack of belief destroy it before reaching its destination."

"But these people go to church regularly, praying all their lives," she said in disbelief.

"Their prayers are wishes, nothing more," said the wizard with a firm voice.

Grace sensed a note of frustration in him.

"For years I have heard them begging for good health, for fortune, for success, for love," continued the wizard. "Always praying for something outside of them to come and fulfill their emptiness. Yet if they would just recognize the strength and light within them, their empty prayers would turn into mighty commands. Then, miracles would flood the earth, uprooting sorrow, doubts and fears, and planting joy and love in their place."

Grace reflected on the wizard's wisdom while curious monarchs crowded around the three. Their master was speaking, and all opened their minds.

"Your prayer was answered because you didn't pray *for* something but prayed *of* something." The wizard resumed his lesson. "You envisioned the positive outcome of your request and felt as though it had already been accepted. No hesitation crept in as you prayed, only trust and belief in the infinite light. Miracles follow any prayer that emerges in this state of mind."

A moment later, the golden butterfly vanished, and the orange cloud of monarchs sang a song of gratitude to him.

Grace sucked in this priceless teaching like heavenly nectar. The strength of the monarch depends on his certainty and confidence in himself. Only a doubtless mind shines with glory and is able to join the eternal light. In the realm of limitlessness, such prayers create wonders all over the good earth. Suddenly, she thought of herself not as a meaningless paperclip insect but as a miracle bearer whose strength could move mountains.

The sun dipped in the west, and the cloud of monarchs scattered into many orange trails. Each flew to a nearby tree to roost for the night. Luxrider and Grace perched on a pine trunk. Soon enough, they were surrounded by hundreds clustered together.

Grace, who always liked her privacy, surprisingly didn't mind her brothers and sisters tight beside her. She became a single orange spot in a glowing carpet and slept like a log. Dawn rose, and she opened her eyes. The others began to wake, shivering their wings. She espied dozens of monarchs still sleeping on the ground. They must have fallen from the tree while dreaming, she chuckled. But when she focused her eyes, her smile turned to dread. What she saw were not bodies on the ground but orange wings, scattered like autumn's dead leaves. Grace shook and shuddered as she stared at the monarch grave-yard.

"What is this death?" she said aloud in a choked voice.

"A hungry mouse," said a sad voice beside her. "We encountered a few in the last week."

She stared at the waking monarchs witnessing the horror with her. They gave bows of respect to their fallen brothers but nothing more. None wept or shuddered. They embraced life with all it threw at them, including death.

Soon enough, Grace found herself accepting the situation. This horror took place, whether I like it or not. I can't change it now, she thought.

When the dawn meditation ended, the butterflies immediately swarmed through the branches and soared high above the pines. A bunch of golden brothers froze in midair, and the orange swarm swirled around them and sang a goodbye song.

They glided for few hours. On her left and right, as far she could see, waves of monarchs flapped their wings and flew to south Texas. After a long while, they landed on a grassy meadow

"You are quiet today," Luxrider stroked her head with his antennae while they enjoyed their break.

Grace said nothing for a while. Then: "Life is short..." she suddenly mumbled. "Death might visit us in any moment."

"That is why a monarch celebrates life in every moment," said Luxrider. "Life is precious. There is no time or need to grieve."

Grace nodded. She had begun to understand how the monarchs find life even in death itself. "We should live each day as though it was our last," she said with twinkling eyes. "Time for more miracles, Luxrider."

Grace soared to the sky with a mischievous smile.

While her brothers and sisters scanned the fields for flowers, Grace's eyes searched for structures. Not homes or apartments, but gigantic buildings where people forgot about their own light. Driven by a new burning purpose, she led her flock through every hospital on their way. Together, they swirled and sang and prayed around the dull buildings, putting them in an orange blaze.

In the following days, none in Texas spoke about the Dallas Cowboys or the Houston Rockets. Politics and business matters had been shoved aside. All they were talking about was the miraculous healings of uncured diseases in hospitals. Time and again, TV channels showed flocks of monarchs flying around hospitals and raising the spirits of people. Incredible stories came from the sick and their families; every heart in every home was moved to tears.

It was as if the Oscar ceremony had abandoned Hollywood and wandered to Texas. Cameras were in the hands of every

Texan; they became regular paparazzi, uploading photos and videos of the orange celebrities around the land.

While all the monarchs glinted like stars, one glowed like a full moon. She was the Oscar winner, the shepherd butterfly that led her flock to where it was needed most. Her prayers turned into commands, and the universe obeyed her with happiness and joy. Not many mastered the language of miracles, yet this little monarch did.

At last, Grace, Luxrider, and the others noticed a mighty chain of mountains to their right and the blue Gulf of Mexico to their left. The day was almost over, so they dived to rest in some mesquite trees. So close to the border, there were signs in English to the north and in Spanish to the south.

"We've reached Mexico..." Grace gasped.

The afternoon sun began to dip, and the wind blew the scattered white clouds, arranging them beside each other like disciplined soldiers. They spread between the mighty Sierra Madres and the sea like an arch, a gateway.

"Well done, sister," said the sun to the wind.

The wind kissed the trees, much pleased. Seldom did she participate in her older sister's art.

"Now, she is ready to work," murmured the wind to the monarchs on the branches.

All gazed in silence.

The sun sent her long golden rays and softly caressed the

arch of clouds. Some turned pink and peach, others red and orange; the middle piece was painted in gold.

A sea of antennae shivered at the magical sight.

"Congratulations, butterflies," announced the sun. "You are about to cross the gate of the monarchs. The last part of your miraculous journey is about to begin. You shall continue south until you see the sign."

The mesquite tree vibrated with excitement as the monarchs flapped their wings and hugged each other.

In the midst of the celebration, the wind blew Grace to one of the top branches that had stood empty. "I am proud of you, child," the wind whispered with a loving voice. "The monarchs have no leader among them, for they are all royalty, kings and queens of the present. Nevertheless, you turned into their shepherd. Unlike humans, they are not attracted to power or charisma; but they will follow love and courage. And you, my Grace, showed these qualities at the highest level."

At last, the young sister left, and Grace gave gratitude for being a part of a miraculous journey.

CHAPTER 17

"Good morning, sleepyhead," Luxrider woke his soul mate with a soft kiss.

Grace opened her eyes and smiled. The sun glimpsed from the east, cuing the flock to begin its first day of flying through Mexico.

After their morning preparation, the orange wave wandered south. They carried with them neither passports nor pesos, just their singing and light. For long days they flew along rivers and villages, curving with the Sierra Madre mountains to their right. Trees appeared less and desert cactuses more, and many monarchs grew tired from the blazing heat. Soon, a tall ridge tunneled the butterfly flock into a narrow gap between mountains and sea.

On the seventh day in Mexico, Grace encountered a crowd of thousands gathered in a town. There was much shouting and commotion going on and people began to throw stones at the police, who had their batons out. Smoke and violence spread and the people of light glowed in blazing furious red. It was the color of anger and fury and hate.

The monarchs, resting in a wood nearby, seemed puzzled and confused.

In a swift decision, Grace flew toward the commotion, but she wasn't alone. An orange army of monarchs was flying beside her, armed with light and prayers.

And so it was that through the canyon of hatred between the two sides flowed a glowing river of love. The monarchs flew back and forth into the gap with songs of peace and visions of harmony. The rocks and curses thrown at the authorities ceased and, in return, the police withdrew their weapons. Soon, the angry red blaze that burned in the people calmed into pink and finally became a soft golden light.

Once again, the monarchs had achieved the impossible, bridging over hate and differences with love.

Grace gave thanks to the universe for accepting her prayer.

"Your request is my command, brave monarch..." a great voice responded.

More days passed and as the butterflies perched on the trees and gazed at the lovely sunset, something new appeared. While the sun still sank behind the Sierra Madre Mountains, her glow didn't diminish. Instead, her golden light first turned orange, then grew into lavender and violet.

"It must be the sign," whispered Luxrider to Grace.

All the monarchs were mesmerized by the sight.

Dusk approached and a sudden column of ultraviolet light pierced the sky like a laser beam. It emerged from a small forest on one of the highest mountain peaks. People could not see the spectacular sight; only the monarchs could see the light. And so they celebrated and laughed and cheered on the branches, eager for the last climb on their miraculous journey.

That night, Grace hardly slept. Adrenaline rushed through her body every time she thought about the journey's end.

Morning came and, with the finish line in sight, the monarchs began the final sprint on their marathon. Above slopes covered with trees and past colorful villages, they flew. Flap, flap, flap, glide.

The locals were ready for their honored guests. Smoke and delicious scents rose from many food stalls. Small shops displayed souvenir shirts, cups, and toys. All had a monarch image on them. A local orchestra played in the packed narrow streets, and all faces seemed happy and smiling.

"They celebrate our arrival," Grace said to Luxrider as they flew around.

The town's cemetery seemed to be the most crowded place. Bouquets of Mexican marigolds covered the white tombs. They were as orange as the monarchs' wings.

As the two landed with their friends, they heard a young

Mexican guide speaking to a group of American tourists in broken English. "Today is the Day of the Dead," he explained. "The locals visit the graves of their deceased loved ones and pray. Some bring the dead's favorite food and drinks, and others carry their pictures. Our elders here believe the monarchs come from a magical world, and they are the souls of their departed ancestors. There is no coincidence these blessed butterflies visit us on the holiday of the dead."

Sunset approached and, while most of their flock had already left the cemetery, Grace and Luxrider stayed.

"Let's spend the night here, my love," whispered Grace to her monarch. "This place is special."

Luxrider craved to reach the mountains, but instead he nodded and hugged his soul mate.

As evening fell, hundreds of candles burned in the graveyard while the locals offered their prayers. In the midst of these, Luxrider and Grace perched on an orange bouquet and scanned the faces around, all of which appeared calm and peaceful.

"What is it, Grace?" asked Luxrider as he caught her sad gaze.

"I don't want this journey to end," she whispered, and placed her head beside him.

"Every journey ends, my love," he sighed. "And the ones who reach it should feel quite fortunate."

"I am afraid of what will happen next; what will happen to us?"

"Trust yourself and the universe," said Luxrider. "You have been blessed with a rare gift. You've been able to join the monarchs' miraculous journey. Look at you now. How much you have learned and changed. You are not the same miserable Grace anymore but transformed into a monarch queen. No one can take that from you. The time has come to fulfill your higher purpose and share all you have learned with your brothers and sisters. You knew this day would come."

Grace nodded. Her tears trickled down upon the orange flowers. "I did," her voice was choked, "but I didn't expect to find my soul mate on the way. The one whose heart beat as one with mine. I would rather live few more months as a monarch and perish in your wings than live dozens of years as a daughter of light."

Luxrider said nothing. He embraced her and her tears covered his body. "True love never dies," he comforted her. "Remember how you lived before, Grace. You owe these lessons and wisdom to your people."

Although she knew he was right, she felt her heart shatter to tiny pieces. She stepped aside and left the warmth of his wings. By the light of many candles, the two lovers slept alone.

CHAPTER 18

Sunrise had been long over when Grace finally opened her eyes. The flowers, pictures of the dead, and melted candles were still there—but not Luxrider. She scanned her surroundings and found no other monarch in the cemetery.

Skipping the morning meditation, she basked in the sun, sipped some nectar and left the town behind. Her mind drifted like the wind on the vast earth. *Where is Luxrider? Why did he leave? Was I selfish last night?* But then she quieted her voice and gazed out at the mountains and the villages. They appeared like rambles of stones under her wings.

Most of all I will miss flying, thought Grace.

Far ahead of her, millions of monarchs formed orange clouds and reached the mountain peaks, more than 10,000 feet high. She trailed only a few hours behind, and her heart boomed like a giant drum.

Some flowers sang from the mountains' green slopes, and

she dived to take her last break. Their nectar tasted heavenly and their songs eased her concerns.

Suddenly, the flowers turned silent as a shadow grew large on the ground. At once, Grace sensed danger and beat her wings, racing into the nearby trees. An orange bird with a black head was chasing her, his mighty beak eager to tear her into pieces. Grosbeak was his name, but the butterflies called him the flying shadow of death. He was a deadly hunter, one of the few birds who could pursue the poisonous monarchs and feast on their bodies. Once pursued by the grosbeak, a monarch had little chance to survive.

"Not now...please...I am so close..." Grace pleaded as she sped through twigs and branches trying to escape. But the persistent shadow was relentless. His beak clanged like two swords clashing.

The hunt drained Grace of her strength and her flight weakened with every moment. Her body began to give in.

The grosbeak was just about to pierce his prize when another monarch appeared on his right and drew his attention.

"You are pretty slow, old man," Luxrider said, egging him on.

The offended bird shrieked and zoomed behind the arrogant butterfly, determined to avenge his pride.

And so Luxrider rushed through dense trees and thorny shrubs to evade his fierce predator.

Grace gasped and hid on a high branch. Her worried eyes followed the deadly chase from afar. Moments later, the bird gave up his ego and his prize and left.

"Luxrider! Luxrider!!" Her voice shivered as she rushed to the thorny brush. Something moved inside and he appeared from the other side of the bush. He flew awkwardly though and sank on the first tree he met.

"Luxrider, you came back to save me," her voice trembled with tears of joy as she landed beside him. "I sensed death closing in on me and almost gave up."

"What's important is that you are alive and safe." His face twisted in pain as he spoke.

"What is wrong, my love..." Grace scanned him with wide eyes, embracing him with her wings.

He twitched and his beautiful right forewing dropped to the ground. She stared in disbelief.

"No!" she sobbed, afraid of touching him now and causing more damage. His remaining three wings were cut and torn. Whatever the shadow of death couldn't do, the spiky shrub had done, slashing Luxrider's body with its thorns.

Luxrider forced a smile to encourage Grace, yet nothing helped. Each part of her shivered. She appeared as a ghostly and lifeless butterfly whose color had turned to a cloak of gray.

"Some bad luck, eh?" he said. "Only a few hours away from journey's end. I wish I could see the wizard's forest and die peacefully."

Grace opened her mouth to uplift his spirit, yet only tears trickled from her eyes. Her blank mind contained no words of comfort, for she knew her beloved soul mate would soar no more.

The sun approached the middle of the sky now, and the two sat beside each other in silence.

"Time to move on, Grace," said Luxrider with a soft voice. "Your journey's end is nearby."

"I am staying with you!!" she answered with a decisive tone.

"I can't fly anymore, my love," he caressed her wings with his antennae. "My journey stops right here. Yet I don't regret it for a moment."

"I won't leave you behind, the same way you didn't abandon me," said Grace and flew high to the top branch.

Luxrider had no strength in him to argue. He closed his eyes instead and fell into a deep sleep. Never before had he felt so weary.

That afternoon, Grace gazed at the heavens and prayed for one last miracle before the end.

The wind came and asked her to continue, saying, "Death is part of life, my daughter."

"You must go on, Grace," said sister sun. "The finish line is at the mountain top. Luxrider risked his life because he believed from the first day that your journey is the most meaningful of all. Don't let him die in vain."

Despite the old sister's counsel, Grace remained in her spot like a statue. She envisioned and sensed Luxrider holding her tight in the Wizard Forest. She had no idea how he would get there; she left that for the infinite wisdom of the universe to figure out. Keeping her focus on the desired outcome cleared her mind from the weeds of doubt. Miracles happen to those who believe in them in the face of adversity.

In the midst of her stillness, she heard a shivering howl; yet it felt more friendly than threatening.

Sunset turned to dusk and the night wore his black cloak. A half-moon glowed, and many diamonds glittered in the sky. Grace gazed at the moon and recalled the night on the cemetery tree when she confessed to Luxrider her real identity.

"You were my witness that night," she whispered to the moon. "That same night I announced my love to my soul mate."

The moon glowed brightly. "I remember the night, Grace," said the moon with a soft voice.

"Do you?" She felt somewhat puzzled, speaking to the moon for the first time.

"Of course I do, monarch," he sounded a bit offended, "for who can forget such a love? You see, Grace, butterflies are ruled by the sun. They depend on her warmth to fly and her light to navigate. Most of them hardly know of my existence, for they are asleep when I climb. The ones who stare at me think I am just another large star. All I can do is caress them with my glow when they sleep. I wish I could hear their songs and carefree laughter."

"Oh, glorious moon," said Grace in genuine awe, "you are no glinting star but the true king of the night. You bring light when all is dark and inspire romance and love among my people."

The moon glowed with pride and joy. "The wolves and the owls and many night hunters give me gratitude. Yet, to hear such a compliment from a monarch is quite rare. It warms my heart."

"Would you bless me with aid to save my true love and soul mate? Of all the others, you, the inspiration of the night, understand me the most," she said, and her wet eyes sparkled under his light.

The moon turned silent and soon hid behind a floating cloud. Then he whispered, "I have no authority to interfere with miracles; only the universe delivers them."

Grace nodded and bowed to the night's king. Then a bright idea came to her lawyerly mind, and she whispered offhandedly, "Songs of glory and wonder would be spread over the land to the savior of my love..."

The moon caught every word and shined with a new desire now. In his vision, monarchs that give gratitude to the sun would praise him also. At last, an opportunity for him to win the old sister's appreciation.

In her heart, Grace knew she had done all in her power. Spending the last night with her soul mate and keeping her belief in his recovery were all that was left.

Luxrider opened his eyes when she landed beside him. He shivered yet beamed at her. She wrapped him with her loving wings and kissed him softly. Soon, his trembling stopped, and both lovers fell asleep.

Sounds of cracking dry leaves awakened Grace. Looking around, she saw nothing except a thick fog. More snaps followed, then ceased. Something sniffed, then scratched the bark ten feet below them. The two monarchs froze.

"Please, not the mice," she prayed, recalling the deadly night when many wings of her friends covered the ground. Neither she nor Luxrider could escape now. The hour was too early and cold for them to move. Instead, they remained in each other's wings, waiting for an inevitable death.

A sudden breeze blew and the tree's lively leaves rustled along with their dead brothers on the ground. Some of the mist dispersed and Grace looked down.

A pair of hazel eyes stared back at her and she almost fell from the branch, such was her surprise. It was none other than a wolf, clad in gray-black fur. He scratched the bark again, nodded, and sat on his back legs, still eyeing the two monarchs.

Luxrider and Grace exchanged stunned glances. Then a memory of the wolf howling and last night's conversation with the moon came to her.

"Of course," she mumbled with glinting eyes. "The moon sent this one..."

Luxrider gaped at her with an open mouth, certain she had lost her wits.

"Come, Luxrider, I think someone is about to give us a ride," her lively voice chuckled. "Trust me," she said, hugging him.

The wounded monarch nodded.

A moment later, the two sank like tangled feathers and landed on the wolf's soft fur.

The young sister laughed, dispersing the fog some more. With the wind at his back, the proud wolf raced up the mountain slopes through pines and firs. Two fortunate passengers gripped his fur and enjoyed the free ride.

"How, Grace..." Luxrider shook his head in disbelief. "What did you do?"

"Nothing...except tempt an old man's pride," she giggled.

"Nothing? Nothing?" The wind's words blew from their backs and the wolf's tail curved forward like an angry scorpion. "She only made the moon do something he'd never done before, interfering beyond his realm. I was there last night, monarch; I heard every word of your conversation."

"When the purpose is just and love spreads out from the heart, everything is possible," Grace announced and gazed at Luxrider beside her.

"Indeed, my daughter," laughed the wind. "No worries. Not a word to my older sister."

Hours later, the fog climbed down to the valleys, and the sun filled the upper slopes with warmth. The two monarchs gaped at the Oyamel fir forest and breathed the crisp fragrance in the air. A sound of rain came, and the wolf halted beside a thick trunk. Grace and Luxrider dug into his fur, trying to find cover. However, no rain dropped from the sky, but an amber river gushed through the trees.

Millions of monarchs were there, some on branches, others on the sunny ground. They painted the forest in orange and black.

"We made it," said Luxrider in disbelief and awe. "We arrived at the wizard's home."

Tears of joy trickled from Grace's eyes and she embraced her soul mate with excitement.

"Gratitude to you, my dear wolf," said Luxrider. "I will forever be in your debt."

To their utmost surprise, the animal stood on his back legs and swirled. The two exchanged a stunned glance. Moments later, Grace hopped onto his muzzle and caressed him with her wings. Her eyes dug into his, and an old loving memory came alive.

"Monasero..." she found herself mumbling.

The wolf bowed, and the two leaped to the ground. He gave them a last smiling gaze and raced back into the trees.

From the millions of flapping wings, a unified pack rushed their way and hovered above the two. They recognized their miraculous shepherds. Joy and happiness grew beyond limits, for the flock had thought they'd lost their two leaders. At once, thousands of monarchs swarmed their wounded brother and carried him to a tree.

When Grace told them about the moon and his noble deed and love, the news spread like fire in a thorn field. Soon songs of praise sounded throughout the region.

That day, the sun climbed in the east while the moon rose in the west. By midday the two sky rulers met.

"Well done, king of the night," the old sister approached him with the utmost respect.

"Thank you, my queen," the moon bowed back. "None can remain idle to the power of love."

CHAPTER 19

Golden sunset fell on the wizard's forest. All the monarchs were roosting on trunks, branches, and twigs. They huddled together and clung to the trees as roots to the ground.

Grace held Luxrider on her right and sank into a deep serenity and stillness. No animal moved, no tree rustled or swayed. The forest fell silent yet it was still very much alive.

Dusk came and washed out the golden color of the day. But instead of introducing the blackness of night, he welcomed an ultraviolet shade. The scent of nectar filled the air.

"Something is about to happen," Grace whispered to Luxrider.

At that moment, a soft voice reached every monarch in the woods. The wizard approached.

"Welcome, my beloved sons and daughters of the monarchs. Thousands of miles you flew and crossed many lands and perils to reach my home. On this miraculous journey many brothers and sisters died, yet their light is forever with us."

Grace exchanged a swift glance with Luxrider, and both bowed to their beloved musketeer brother, Monasero.

"Here, on these magical trees, you shall rest and grow wise until spring arrives," the wizard went on. "I followed each one of you from birth. Watching your early caterpillar's life, I held your hands through the transformation stage in the chrysalis. At last, you turned into butterflies, and my light traveled with you across distant lands. However, none of you heard my real tale. As a gracious host, I would like to share with you an old journey of mine."

The monarchs shifted their wings with excitement and expectation.

"My story began thousands of years ago in a village down on the slopes of this forest. I was a young man at the time, not yet past twenty. Having fallen deeply in love with a lady who agreed to become my wife, I felt the most fortunate man on earth. Our blissful hearts beat as one, and the world appeared to me like a perfect dream. Yet, like any fantasy bubble, it burst into a harsh reality.

"One morning, I woke up, but she didn't. Dead, she lay in my arms, taken from me forever. Pain and agony lashed my heart and tortured me constantly. Soon, I became angry and hateful, blaming the cruelty of life; I cursed everything on my way. Grief and despair dragged me to rock-bottom and I decided to end my miserable existence.

"As I hung myself on one of these forest trees, a flash of light cut the rope and dropped me to the ground. Then, a blanket of white light wrapped my cold body and a soft voice spoke inside my head.

"'Why do you want to kill yourself?' The voice asked. 'Life is miserable,' I answered. 'I lost my only love and happiness. Nothing is left for me except burning pain. I desire to live no more.'

"The voice fell into silence, then whispered: 'True love is never lost. What would you do to get her beside you once again?' he asked me, and I sensed a spark of hope tingling in my heart.

"'I would do anything!' I replied without hesitation. 'Can you do it? Can you bring her back?'

"'I am about to offer you something precious,' he said to me. 'Yet know this: life is a perfect exchange. You can't get something for nothing. I want light for a light.' I didn't grasp his meaning, so he explained. 'I am willing to get you back the light of your wife, but you must create another light first.'

"Without even knowing the voice's plan, I agreed at once. And so this pure white blanket entered my body, and I was no more a man but light without a form. Limitless and everywhere. The world turned into a magical place, and I sensed the aliveness of every tree and flower, every animal and person. The wind and sun answered my call, and the universe my command.

"Moments later the voice spoke again. 'There is a small creature, an insignificant insect to the eye, which lives in utter darkness. Rarely and only by luck does it fulfill its destiny and become a butterfly. Your task is to guide these orphan caterpillars through their transformation until they turn into butterflies.'

"For long moments, I said nothing. Finally, I asked, 'Do you want me to teach an insect? Why is this so important?'

"'This is no regular bug,' answered the voice. 'These bugs are kings and queens in the making. A day will come when they will accomplish their purpose and transform into butterflies. Their light and grace will impact everything in the world. On delicate wings they will carry love and in their hearts, miracles. I call them the flowers of heaven, for when they flap their colorful wings and float in midair that is what they look like. Yet no roots tie them to the ground. These carefree flowers are my chosen children. Their glowing light and fragrance will rouse the people from their sleep and cast out darkness forever.'

"A moment later, he vanished. Right there, I accepted the task with faith and urgency, for I realized the difference I could make. And so my adventure and journey as the butterflies' teacher had begun.

"At first, I became a student and studied their change carefully. I followed the egg, the young caterpillar, and the chrysalis. Soon, I spoke to the few butterflies that had made the transformation and learned much more. After long observation, I noticed that many of the eggs were eaten before they hatched. The caterpillars that did manage to come out faced hunting ants, spiders, and birds. Those that survived these challenges turned into chrysalises. Yet most did not endure the transformation. Their greatest enemy was the fear of change.

"They would panic and scream in pain and despair, inviting predators to devour them.

"I began to guide them through the process, teaching them to confront their fears. I gave them visions of hope and strength-ened their belief in what they might become. As the months had passed, more eggs survived. Many more caterpillars reached the chrysalis stage and a thousand times more turned into but-terflies.

"Soon enough, drifting flowers of numerous colors glided in the air and awakened the spark of light in people's hearts.

"I became father to all butterflies. Yet it was you, orange monarch, with whom I had the strongest bond. After the trans-formation, I continued to be your master. While the other but-terflies seemed carefree and not interested to learn more than needed, you monarchs were quite different. Your curiosity and desire to transform have no boundaries. Your wisdom contin-ues to grow and golden light radiates from your wings. And for that, you deliver the greatest butterfly effect.

"One fall day the voice visited me again. He seemed much pleased with the work I had done and the number of butterflies roaming the land. As he promised, my beloved wife returned as an eternal light beside me, and so we came back to dwell in this forest.

"At the end of my first autumn here, flocks of monarchs flew among the trees. I was stunned to discover they had journeyed thousands of miles from the north and followed my trails of light. 'We came to learn more about love and transformation,' they said. This was the first class of your ancestors, and I shared with them much knowledge about life.

"In spring and summer, I helped many other caterpillars to transform into butterflies. I was fascinated by their will to change and learn and, as much as I taught them, I became their avid student.

"But for dozens of centuries only the brave monarchs of fall have embarked on a miraculous journey to the south and to my home.

"Open your minds and hearts, my beloved butterflies, and knowledge and eternal peace shall be yours."

The wizard's voice faded, but when Grace glanced into the forest, her heart stopped. A man figure made of bright white light strolled among the trees. Beside him, holding his hand, walked a lady of light. The branches above swayed and the wind whistled a loving tune.

"Luxrider! Look, my love. It's the wizard and his precious wife," Grace said with glossy eyes gazing at the majestic couple.

Luxrider said nothing.

She stared at her soul mate and found him frozen in his spot. When she touched him with her wing, he dropped like a lifeless leaf until he met the ground.

Luxrider, the love of her life, was no more.

CHAPTER 20

G race opened her eyes, but the bright light around her was so intense, she shut them again. At first, she had no idea what had happened; then, as the last memory came to her, tears gushed from her eyes and forced them open. Luxrider, her soul mate, was gone.

In a mist of a dazzling white glare, she kept moving—yet didn't fly. Soon enough, Grace realized she stood on the wizard's shoulder, strolling with him among the trees.

"Hello, monarch," he said to her with his calm voice.

She said nothing, afraid her tears would run like the Niagara Falls.

"Luxrider has joined his golden brothers and sisters," said the wizard.

"I know," Grace said, her voice choked in grief.

For long minutes, he wandered in the woods, yet neither of them spoke.

Grace stared through blurred eyes at the branches and trunks covered with monarchs. All had found warmth and comfort in each other's wings, but not her. No wings could wrap around her like Luxrider's.

Though the sun had already risen, the forest seemed asleep.

"What happened to me?" Grace broke the silence.

"You fainted and fell," smiled the glowing man, "all the way down into my hand."

"Thank you," she mumbled. "How did you bear this terrible pain, my wizard? Losing the one you loved?"

"At first, I barely survived," he answered. "The more I battled my depression, the more it grew into a monster. Hopeless, I attempted to end my useless life until the light came to me and showed me the truth."

"What did he show you?" asked Grace, remembering his remarkable story.

"My vision transformed as the light entered my mind—and so did the world around me. The forest, which seemed dim before, was flooded by the most beautiful light. Love shined over trees, flowers, and animals, spreading in abundance. Nothing actually changed in the forest, only in my mind," said the wizard.

"It was your pain and grief that kept you in darkness, blocking from you the sight of truth," Grace pondered out loud.

"That is right, my daughter," said the man, pleased. His

light dazzled like the midday sun. "My gloomy mind showed me a dark reality outside. But as the light stepped in and cast the shadows from my mind, the world bloomed with wonder. Seeing the abundant vivid light, I knew love exists forever; only its form changes. True love can never be lost. That realization comforted me much and planted new hope. When the voice challenged me to help caterpillars transform into butterflies, I found joy again. I turned into a wizard much as the caterpillars change into butterflies.

"Soon enough, the monarchs' journey south began to awaken the people from their sleep. You see, Grace, when I accepted the task, I was nothing but a man who desired to bring back his lost love and fulfill his emptiness. But being on a journey of my own and witnessing the transformations and miracles around changed me forever. Soon I forgot my loss. Instead, my mind dwelled on the love around me. Butterflies scattered in millions and carried with them hope and joy on the land.

"Yet my biggest pride is the monarchs, for their hearts beat with courage and their desire to transform is second to none. They understand their transformation doesn't end in flying but in becoming a butterfly, the one who carries the light. That is why they create miracles among the people. That is why their journey and survival are as significant as the people themselves."

Grace devoured his wisdom for long minutes, and peace

came to her mind. "Tell me what I must do, my wizard, for you are bright and wise like no other," she said.

"I can't tell you that," replied the master. "All I can do is teach and guide you. The journey you choose is yours to travel."

"I don't know what I am anymore," mumbled Grace. "A monarch? A woman?"

"You are a light. Never forget that!" the wizard said with a firm voice. "Whatever form you want to play with is up to you, and is much less significant than your essence. All power and joy come to the one who knows himself beyond his form. Nevertheless, if your mind is not clear yet, remain here in the forest with your brothers and sisters until you identify your path."

"Thank you," said Grace, ready to fly back to her tree.

"Good luck, monarch," a soft lady's voice spoke from the other shoulder.

Grace stared with utter astonishment at a snow white butterfly standing on the wizard's left shoulder. She hadn't noticed her until now.

"Who are you?" Grace's voice trembled.

"I am the wizard's wife and soul mate," smiled the snowy butterfly.

"You turned into a butterfly..."

"Remember this important lesson, my child," said the wizard. "True love is never lost. Light is light beyond any shape and form."

With that said, the monarch flew away. When she turned her head, the white butterfly gave a kiss to her husband, and new hope rushed through Grace's heart.

CHAPTER 21

Fall turned into winter and the days and nights grew cold. On the Oyamel branches, flocks of monarchs embraced each other and kept still. The trees gave warmth and protected them from the cold, yet not from predators.

Mice feasted on the orange clusters and birds hunted them down. But the monarchs remained in their spots. A few times the hunters pierced the butterflies beside Grace. They came so close to her she could sense a mouse tail brushing her once and crumbles of wings dropping on her face. Nonetheless, she stayed calm. Death became part of life and troubled her much less.

During these months, Grace sank into a profound serenity. Life seemed simple now, and wisdom and light spilled from her.

Soon, winter was packing his chill air, and the wind carried some pleasant breezes into the forest. The monarchs were ready to find their soul mates and travel north to Texas, where they would lay eggs and die.

One night, as the moon shone above the trees, Grace made her final decision.

Dawn rose on the wizard's home, and Grace shivered. That morning, however, she sensed a different kind of shivering. She tried to flap her orange wings, but nothing moved. Instead, goosebumps marched on her smooth skin like an army of ants. She opened her eyes and gasped. She was a monarch no more but a woman, a bare naked one.

The damp grass on the ground chilled her body. She tried to cover herself with her hands, but there was too much to hide. A sense of shame she had forgotten about crept in.

"What am I supposed to do now?" she mumbled to herself and stood, scanning around for any curious eyes. She didn't dare call the wizard for help.

The forest and the monarchs seemed quite idle to the naked stranger—all except one tree.

Despite the early hour, Grace's flock shifted their wings and swayed in their spots. New rays of sun caressed them, and soon enough they began to fly.

Grace, who hid helplessly behind a trunk, sensed an orange and black swarm to her left. Moments later, the monarchs landed on her chilled skin and formed a majestic dress. Tears of joy

rolled down her cheeks as she gaped at her lively garment. Butterflies covered her from breast to ankles. Her hands and arms,
however, remained exposed, as did the upper part of her back.
As she stepped away from the tree, the royal dress inflated and
shrank with her motion as though it was made of soft silk.

*If I had married Luxrider, this would have been my wed-
ding gown*, she thought sadly. A prickle on her ears and around
her neck caught her attention as she noticed she was wearing a
monarch necklace and earrings.

Grace spun like a girl at her first prom, and the monarchs
followed her movement to perfection. She laughed and swung
her amber hair in disbelief.

Suddenly, a butterfly left her necklace, landed on her hand
and coiled his antennae around her finger. "How do you like
your dress, Grace?" he asked her.

"I love it!! Thank you!!" she beamed at him. "You all have
your own journey to take now, and you should prepare your-
selves to leave."

"You led us through part of our journey and showed us the
way of miracles like no other. Now we shall follow you and
clad your body until our service is needed no more," said the
monarch.

"But..." said Grace and a voice cut her short.

"No but," said the wizard as he approached from behind.
"Take your flock's advice and begin your new journey with

them. Have no fear, my daughter; you made the right choice."

Grace gazed at the wizard for the first time as a woman sees a man. He was tall and broad in the shoulders. White hair fell upon his back, as pure as the first snow on a mountain peak. Wisdom emanated from each groove on his forehead, yet his face appeared timeless and was lit by two glinting sapphire eyes.

She bowed to him opened-mouthed.

"You look marvelous, my daughter," he smiled. "Go now and change the world."

He vanished with roaring laughter before she could say a word.

Grace gasped. "Change the world?" Her old cynical voice repeated the wizard's words in disbelief. She was in a foreign country, clothed in a monarch dress that might leave her at any moment. Yet he asked her to do the impossible.

But then memories of the mighty miracles she had performed flooded her mind. The wisdom within her woke up.

"In my right state of mind I did the unthinkable. I must trust myself and the universe no matter what," she whispered. "I did not pass through this miraculous journey, learn precious lessons, and perform wonders only to return to the old me. Shut up and be gone, old voice, you are part of the new Grace no more."

Her will and clear intent flashed like lightning and shattered her doubtful voice to dust. The power dwelling in her now could move mountains, for she was a daughter of light with a transformed mind. One who might ask—and would receive.

She stepped on the dirt path, and her feet relished the touch of the ground. The forest seemed abundant with life, and the singing birds, no longer a threat, now seemed delightful. She had no idea what direction to take. At last, she decided to go down the mountain slopes on a winding trail.

Half an hour later, the sound of axes and saws came from the right. Grace froze. Faint human voices reached her. She left the path, striding among the ancient pines and Oyamel firs. All of a sudden, her monarch dress quivered and so did her heart, for they all sensed sadness around them. Something moved ahead and she pressed forward.

Five donkeys stared at her with miserable eyes, for each had a pile of logs bound to his back. Next to them, men were cutting giant trees into pieces.

Tears ran down Grace's cheeks, and every blow of an ax made her bones shudder.

Suddenly, one man who had his ax high above his head caught a glimpse of the strange woman. For a moment, his tanned face turned pale and his hands froze. Then, the ax dropped to the ground as its owner pointed at Grace with a shaking finger.

His friends turned around and gaped at the lady covered with butterflies.

"Bruja mariposa..." Their trembling voices grew into terrified screams. "Bruja mariposa!!"

The Butterfly Witch stood still with her monarchs while the seven men dropped their axes and saws and, screaming, fled through the forest.

For a while, Grace stared at the logging area in disbelief: so many of the proud trees of wonder that safeguarded the monarchs and had been their home for centuries were now only shallow stumps.

Moments later, she grabbed a saw and cut the ropes from the poor donkeys. The piles of logs rolled to the ground and the puzzled animals, now feeling light as a feather, rushed back to the trail. Grace followed them, hoping to find people who might help her. Barefoot, she walked over the twisting path. Before long, the sound of distant bells reached her ears.

"Gong...Gong...Gong..."

"The village must be close by," she encouraged herself, for her feet ached and her head spun under the hot sun.

"Gong...Gong...Gong..." the bells continued to ring and between their loud calls she caught voices of people. Grace's heart raced as she rounded a curve in the dirt road and spotted the first village homes.

A colorful crowd of a few thousand buzzed like a beehive. Then, as the lady with the monarch dress appeared around the corner, all fell silent. Jaws dropped; eyes popped as she stood still gazing at them—and they gazed at her

"Reina mariposa...Reina mariposa..." the voices murmured with excitement.

Some little girls dressed in a monarch costume rushed to Grace and surrounded her with open mouths. Suddenly, the mesmerized crowd parted like the Red Sea and through them a column of short ladies passed. They wore colorful traditional dresses and carried baskets of fruit on their heads. Their coal black hair was tightened into long ponytails, and orange flowers wrapped around their necks. These were the indigenous Mazahua people who had lived in those mountains for thousands of years.

The Mazahua ladies stood on both sides of the road and gazed at the crowd. An old woman supported by two boys plodded up the steep climb and halted in front of Grace. She scanned the butterfly lady and her old dry eyes flowed with tears; her dry, barren skin gulped them as the desert drinks the rain. The old woman bent to bow but Grace stepped forward and held her by the hands, not letting her do so. Instead, the two women's foreheads met. Tears dripped from Grace's eyes as well. She looked at the old woman and sensed her long-dead mother's presence once again. Kindness and love radiated from the old woman's eyes and stirred her heart.

Moments later, the old lady turned to the tense faces of the villagers. Wiping away her tears, she announced, "Monarca

Reina!!"

At once, the people cheered and music played. Two little girls dressed in orange and black grabbed Grace's hands and pulled her to walk behind the Mazahua women.

Grace's heart boomed like a thunderstorm as the procession passed ogling eyes and open mouths. For a full hour they all marched through the narrow streets of the small town. Monarch paintings and banners decorated homes and stores. Grace felt stunned as she strolled, forgetting herself in this dreamy celebration.

"Today is the monarch festival," a smiling girl said to her in broken English.

At last, they reached a plaza with a tall church in its center and the crowd surrounded Grace. The old woman took her hand and led Grace to one of the homes nearby. While none followed the two, all eyes remained on them as they entered the little house.

Red Spanish tiles covered the floors, and the walls were painted yellow. Wooden beams stretched along the living room ceiling. The scent of tortillas baking filled the air.

Grace only glanced at her surroundings briefly before her eyes fell on a statue of a woman clothed in a monarch dress. It was the most majestic garment she had ever seen. Without will, her feet compelled her forward.

The old woman wore a mysterious smile as she scurried

to open the two arched windows. Then, without a word, she removed the stunning dress from the ancient statue and handed it to Grace.

As though it was a sign, the monarch flock that had kept her body covered and protected since leaving the mountain top flew off her. They swirled as bees around their beloved queen and then zoomed out through the open windows.

The excited murmurs of the crowd outside turned into cheers as they witnessed the orange butterflies soaring out of the house.

Grace, feeling embarrassed at her nakedness, quickly donned the monarch dress.

The wrinkles on the old lady's forehead shimmered like threads of gold. She clapped her hands and pointed at the floor. A colorful embroidered rug was spread under Grace's feet. There were green mountains and a winding path climbing down that reached a village.

Grace's heart froze. Where the path met the village homes, a crowd of people gathered and all stared at a naked woman covered with monarchs.

"La profecia..." The old woman pointed at Grace and her eyes glittered like two stars.

CHAPTER 22

W hen Grace came out of the old woman's home wearing the ancient monarch dress, the people's hearts stopped. Young and old, they all knew the prophecy: one day a monarch queen in human form would arrive and spread blessings and wisdom throughout the land. Nevertheless, witnessing their ancestors' legend come alive before their very eyes stirred emotions in them like erupted volcanoes. Stunned girls watched their mothers and fathers shed tears of joy. Those who found their tongues mumbled in awe, "Monarca Reina... Monarca Reina..." Trumpets played, drums banged, and a monarch festival like none history had ever seen began.

Grace joined the people in dances she didn't know and sang songs in a language she didn't understand, yet her heart bloomed with joy. *Love has neither boundaries nor borders*, she thought.

The usual two-day monarch festival in Angangueo lasted a week that year. Rumors of the butterfly queen spread throughout the region and people traveled from many villages and towns to see the ancient legend come true.

Grace grew tired of the many visitors but she remained polite. There were no moments of silence left for her, something she had cherished when she was a butterfly.

At last, the festival ended, and she found herself climbing the road to one of the monarchs' sanctuaries. Crisp forest air greeted her as she gazed at the remaining butterflies. She rubbed her cheeks against a pine trunk. His rough bark grazed her skin but comforted her heart, reviving the long days she had perched on him beside her flock. Moments later, she sat on the cool ground and rested, falling into a deep sleep. Mixed dreams of Grace the woman and the monarch tangled in her mind and the clarity she had hoped for didn't come. Coming back down the hill, her mind drifted and she felt more lost than ever.

The days turned into weeks and the weeks into months, and the town's homes and residents grew familiar. She recalled many by name and the people honored and embraced her with much love. They brought her gifts of clothing and other necessities. Many pleaded with her to dwell in their homes and bless them with her presence, yet she chose to stay with the old lady. Every day, the owners of restaurants and local cafes sent invitations to her to dine at their places. At first Grace accepted, but as time went by her restlessness increased, and she preferred to be alone.

"What should I do now? Why are there no signs for me? How am I to fulfill my purpose?" she had asked herself over and over.

Long hours she sat with a notebook and pen, trying to record the wisdom of her miraculous journey. The lessons of the wizard and the wind and the sun and all she had experienced stirred in her mind like a boiling soup, splashing all around. Yet whatever she managed to write she scratched out at once. Grace simply couldn't find a way to express her wisdom.

Frustration built in her; like one of the stray dogs, she wandered the streets of Angangueo. Soon, the queen of the present moment began to dwell on her past. More and more she recalled her monarch journey and the liveliness she felt by living so fully in the present moment. She had carried miracles and light wherever she flew. Life was indeed precious and full of purpose then.

The long days of summer shortened, and the cool breeze of fall stroked the high mountains slopes. Sweet air spread throughout the town. Early flocks of monarchs traveled through the streets and peacefulness knocked on the hearts of the people.

When the day of the dead arrived, Grace joined her new friends in the local cemetery. Each family carried pictures, some candles, and the favorite food of the deceased, placing these items on their tombs.

Grace gazed from a distance. A full year had passed since she had landed with Luxrider in this graveyard, yet it seemed like a lifetime.

Grace had no graves to set candles upon for her beloved ones. So instead, she sent her genuine love toward the glinting stars, praying they would carry the message to all.

A golden dawn rose, and Grace woke up beneath an avocado tree near the cemetery. On a tomb beside her, two monarchs embraced each other and basked under the soaring sun. Her heart played a gentle tune as she, in utter stillness, gazed at them. At once, she joined them in a morning meditation. Since the day she had turned back into being human, she had forgotten all about her dawn practice. Now, she dived into that realm of tranquility—and the world appeared magical again.

After a while, Grace opened her eyes. Every cell in her body danced to a blissful tune. The two butterflies that had stood on the tomb were now perched on her hands. They licked the dampness from her skin, and it tingled. For a long minute, and for no particular reason, Grace roared with laughter.

It was no regular laugh but one that rose from the depth of her soul. A healing glee; all of her concerns dissolved, troubling her no more. She kissed the butterflies and wished them a successful journey's end. They flew off, and Grace jumped to her feet with new liveliness. The fogginess of her mind had begun to clear away.

When she stepped into the town plaza, it was buzzing with people. Mr. Gomez, one of the café owners, spotted her through the window and rushed to her with her favorite cappuccino.

"Good morning, Señorita Grace," he smiled at her.

She grinned and kissed him on his cheeks. "Nothing is comparable to your cappuccino, Señor Gomez," she winked at him. "You mix your coffee with love!"

The man blushed like a plum and went on explaining how important it is to use purified water, and grind the coffee beans and...

However, Grace lost him completely. Not because he bored her but because her hazel eyes gaped at some familiar faces.

A few tables away, a family of three crowded around a small table. They were a couple in their forties with their young daughter. The cappuccino shook in her hand, and the foam threatened to spill as she stared at the girl.

Brian, the father, kissed his wife's hand while his daughter was painting on a white board. "The Texan family," Grace mumbled to herself. Her legs pulled her to the table, leaving Mr. Gomez talking to himself.

"Hello..." said the wife, darting a suspicious glance at the strange woman.

"Good morning," answered Grace, embarrassed. "I am sorry, I confused you with friends." She didn't know what else to say and that was the first thing that came to mind.

"Actually, you seemed familiar also," smiled the lady.

The girl gazed at Grace for the first time and nodded. None spoke for some moments.

"We came here to visit the monarchs' sanctuary in the mountains," smiled the wife. "My name is Amy, and this is my husband Brian and my daughter Emily."

"It's more than just a visit, Mom," said the brunette girl at once, giving her mother an offended stare. "We came to thank them for saving my father..."

The man smiled and shrugged his shoulders, and his wife measured Grace's face, ready to dismiss her daughter's comment.

"Monarchs...saving your father?" Grace beamed at Emily. "I would love to hear such a story."

Before her parents could say a word, the girl told Grace all about her father's accident and the prayer in the church and how thousands of monarchs stormed inside and swirled around the people. "Then the phone rang and they told us Daddy was alright," chuckled Emily.

Grace said nothing, but her eyes twinkled at the girl. Emily's blue eyes sparkled back. Then she opened her watercolor pad and leafed through drawings and paintings until she stopped.

"You see, Miss? I didn't lie." She invited Grace to take a look.

The blood drained from Grace's face as she gaped at a painting of the monarchs flying in the church. Emily turned over a page and Grace recognized herself as a monarch sitting on the girl's hand.

"This butterfly is my hero," the daughter laughed. "She was the first one to fly and only later the others came."

Tears dropped on the paper and the couple exchanged a stunned glance. Grace kissed the young girl on her forehead and stroked her hair.

"Thank you for sharing this incredible story, Emily," she mumbled. "I hope you will continue painting."

"Always," nodded the girl with determined eyes.

A moment later, Grace said goodbye to the family and rushed back to the old lady's home. She now knew exactly what to do next.

CHAPTER 23

It was 8 a.m. when Grace stuffed her few belongings into a handmade Mexican backpack. The monarch dress was folded on her bed. She slid her fingers over the soft fabric and said goodbye to the wonderful memories she had in Angangueo. A week had passed since she told the old lady of her decision to leave the town. The Mazahua woman just smiled at her and nodded, as though she knew the day would come.

The baking scent of cakes and fried eggs came from the kitchen and Grace sighed. Her lips quivered at the thought of leaving the good old woman. Of everyone, she would miss her the most. The delicious aroma of her cooking and the sound of her rolling laughter had become a significant part of Grace's new life. However, she couldn't ignore the omens she had seen. The meeting with Emily and her family was no coincidence. It paved a clear path to an uncertain future. "I am going to paint again," she promised herself that day. "From now on, I will only do what I am passionate about."

She left her room and passed by the nude statue. A smile curled her lips as she recalled the moment her monarchs left her naked and the old woman handed her the dress.

"Take care of the monarchs," Grace whispered to the naked lady, and put the dress back on her.

In the kitchen, the old woman and her granddaughter sat around the table and smiled at her. Her favorite vegetable omelet and fruit salad waited near her empty chair. Tears trickled down Grace's cheeks as she gazed at the two, and she stood frozen like a glacier.

With a big smile, the Mazahua lady got up and hugged her warmly, then led her to sit beside her to enjoy her last hearty breakfast...

Saying goodbye turned out to be harder than Grace had thought. At the door, they embraced again, and the old lady kissed her on the forehead.

"Monarca Reina," she said and wiped the tears from Grace's eyes.

At last, Grace opened the door—but her stunned feet refused to step beyond the threshold. Hundreds of faces crowded the streets and all eyes were upon her.

The butterfly queen finally headed outside. Many people reached out to her, wishing her success and luck on her new journey. At the plaza, beside the tall church, the mayor was waiting. The old man with the white cowboy hat greeted her with a sad smile, handing her a flower and an envelope.

"This is for you, my Grace, from all the townspeople," he said in his thickly accented English.

It was a thick stack of hundred peso bills.

"No...No...I can't have it..." She shook her head, and her hazel eyes turned wet again.

"Please, my dear," said the mayor and hugged her. "You will honor us."

"This is too much..." She wiped her tears.

"Your coming was a blessing to Angangueo, to all of us."

"I didn't do anything," Grace said quite genuinely.

"Anything?" chuckled the old man. "You brought us miracles, one after the other.

People came from far places to our town because they heard of your story. Our hotels and motels were booked for months ahead, and the shops and restaurants prospered like never before. Your tale reached the local governor even, and he promised to stop the illegal logging once and for all. But above all, our people witnessed an ancient legend come true in front of our own eyes. How many people can say that? You gave us more than you could ever imagine."

The mayor accompanied her to a taxi, and the Mazahua women threw golden flowers behind her.

"Señorita Grace! Señorita Grace!" called a man from

behind, rushing through the crowd.

Mr. Gomez panted and handed her a cup. "Your cappuccino...exactly the way you like it..."

Tears flowed like mountain streams on Grace's face as she hugged the kind man. She could barely mumble a thank you, so she just nodded and smiled. Without a word, she got into the cab. Through the window, she found the twinkling eyes of the old woman and sent her a butterfly kiss. A moment later the taxi raced toward Mexico City.

The people at the Canadian embassy were very helpful and issued her a new passport within days.

"We are terribly sorry for what you have been through, Grace," a young lady said to her. "It must have been a horrible experience."

Grace nodded with a sad face. She had had to lie and tell them she had been robbed and lost all of her documents. Who would have believed that she crossed the border as a monarch?

Now, she was on her way to the airport, ready to fly home. Grace was standing in line to buy a ticket to Toronto when her eyes met a glowing banner.

"Ten-day cruise from Puerto Vallarta to Vancouver along the Mexican Riviera & Pacific Coastal. Our luxurious 'Light Rider' ship will take you on a magical voyage all the way to Canada for only $1,099."

Grace's heart thundered and her mouth dropped open.

"Light Rider..." she mumbled.

"Miss...Señorita..." called a woman behind the counter, sounding quite annoyed.

"Sorry..." apologized Grace with a smile. "Do you know by any chance if I can get on this cruise?" She pointed at the banner.

"One moment, please," said the lady and checked the screen on her computer.

What are you doing? her doubting voice nagged. *Because you noticed the words "light rider" you're about to change your destination? Stupid, Grace!*

"The ship leaves tomorrow from Puerto Vallarta," the woman cut her thoughts. "The last flight to Puerto Vallarta leaves in two hours. Would you like to buy a ticket?"

Without hesitation, ignoring her doubts and once again trusting her intuition, Grace answered, "Yes!"

The morning of the day after came and Grace went aboard a gigantic ship, set to sail all the way to Canada. Her cabin was spacious and included a small private balcony facing the sea. As she put away her few things, she thanked the beloved people of Angangueo, whose generous help made it possible for her to return to her home; how else would she have done so?

She spent most of her time at sea on the open decks, feeling the wind and the sun not only on her skin but in her bones and every cell in her body. The vast blue ocean soothed her mind and she sank deeper and deeper into his stillness.

Day and night, Grace carried her watercolor block and kit, painting every vision that came to mind. Even when the Light Rider docked at harbors and the passengers debarked to visit the places, Grace stayed on board to paint. She melted into her art and the joy radiated from her eyes.

On the ninth day of the voyage, a lady joined her at lunch. "Are you coming to the ball tonight?" she asked.

"I don't think so," said Grace, "I want to finish one of my paintings."

"I've seen you all over the ship with your art board," said the woman. "I wish I had something to be so passionate about."

"Listen to your heart and you shall find it," smiled Grace and left the table to visit the upper deck.

The sun dove into the blue sea and brushed the horizon with red and gold. Grace closed her eyes and soaked in the depths of the Pacific Ocean, giving gratitude for all the experiences she had gone through. As darkness came, she went down to her cabin to paint. A full moon was still glowing with all his might when she completed her painting. She went out to her little balcony to hold the block under his light. On it two butterflies in silhouette kissed each other on a branch under a shining moon.

"I will never forget your kind deed, king of the night," she smiled at him. Then she went back into her room, smiling and proud of herself. The painting looked remarkable, even to her critical eyes.

Ready to retire, she pulled a pair of pajamas from her bag, but a different fabric touched her fingers; a soft one that gave her a shiver. Grace drew it out and her heart froze: she was holding the stunning monarch dress.

"How?" she mumbled. Then the mischievous smile on the old Mazahua lady's face came to her memory. "You sneaky old one..." she shook her head and chuckled. The clock on the wall showed 9 p.m. The night was still young, she thought, and rushed into the shower.

The music from the ballroom sounded louder as she approached the lobby where the elevators were. Grace stood in her monarch dress, striking and glowing like a real butterfly queen.

A lady in uniform came out of an elevator and her eyes popped as she scanned Grace from head to toe. "Where do you think you are going like this?" she snapped and grabbed Grace by the arm.

"To the ball..." Grace mumbled in a soft voice.

"No...No...No...No way...not like this! Just wait here! Don't move!" said the nosy lady.

Grace froze in her place, afraid to take a step. Perhaps there is a dress code, she thought, and felt stupid. Moments later, when the lady had not returned, she decided to return to her room. She'd taken but a few steps into the corridor when an irritating voice came from behind.

"Hey, princess, where are you going? Come back here." It was the uniformed woman, who rushed over to Grace and kneeled.

Grace stared at her in disbelief.

"Remove your shoes, please," said the woman, who then placed Grace's feet into elegant black high heels. "That's more like it. Now you look like a monarch queen!"

Grace's face turned red. She hadn't even thought about the fact that she had been wearing flip flop sandals. "Thank you." She beamed at the lady.

"You are most welcome, butterfly." The staff member winked at her. "Enjoy your dancing."

Grace smiled and gracefully strolled into one of the elevators, feeling like royalty. When the doors opened she stepped into the ample ballroom. Hundreds of people crowded the place. Many were sitting around tables while others circled the dance floor upon which dozens of couples floated to the rhythm of a waltz.

It wasn't long before many eyes fell upon the graceful monarch queen. Lips parted, ladies murmured, and men's necks twisted like ropes as their gazes followed Grace to her seat. But she paid no heed to them. Her gaze was upon the spinning couples and the magical world of ballroom dancing. When she was in her early twenties she had a real knack for it.

"May I?" A voice shook her from her memories and a man's hand reached forward.

"I'd love to!" Grace smiled and followed the older man to the dance floor.

After they waltzed, he escorted her back to her table. Immediately a young fellow invited her for the rumba. Then another grabbed her for the cha-cha, then a mambo with another. Grace was having the time of her life.

After two hours of nonstop dancing and much sweat, she finally had to say no thank you. She walked back to her table to catch her breath. She'd almost forgotten about the pain that comes with high heels; her feet craved relief. As she bent down to take off her shoes, an Argentine tango played. Her heart skipped a beat, for it was her favorite dance. She recalled how rare it was to find a good tango dancer, one who could be in sync with his partner in such a way that the lady felt like a cloud floating in heaven.

Suddenly, elegant black shoes appeared in front of her. Grace's eyes traveled up a pair of gray suit pants and jacket and a black button shirt. When she met his grey-blue eyes glinting at her from his tanned face, a sensation of heat rushed through her body. At once, she found herself putting the high heels back on her feet; miraculously, there was no pain.

The man looked to be in his late thirties; a few silver strands glimpsed from his short black hair. He smiled and, without a word, extended his hand.

The two walked to the dance floor. Such was the glow they created, the cheeks of the ladies watching turned green underneath their makeup and the men felt hot under their collars.

Grace melted into the stranger's strong embrace, her breasts pressed against his muscular chest. And so the tango began. Their hearts shared beats and the tango went on and on into timelessness. Never before had Grace danced with such a dancer. His lead was sharp as a razor; she never had to think of what to do but just did.

When the music at last ended, the two remained in their embrace on the floor. Neither cared about each other's name, what they did for a living, where they were from—only that precious moment mattered.

Finally, their bodies and their smiling cheeks separated.

"Would you care for a walk under the stars?" His voice sounded deep yet warm.

She nodded with sparkling eyes, and they left the ballroom for the night's fresh air.

"My name is Grace, by the way," she said as they strolled the upper deck.

"Grace, the monarch," he whispered with a mischievous smile and kissed her hand. "It's a pleasure. My name is Leo. Leo Lichtknecht."

"Licht..." she tried to repeat it, and he laughed.

"I know... I know... No one can say the damn name. It's Dutch. My great grandparents immigrated to Vancouver long ago and left me stuck with this name."

Grace giggled and felt she was talking to a long-time friend.

"You may be surprised, but it actually has a meaning," he said. "It means the knight of light...or the light rider, as far as I remember. Quite dramatic, don't you think?"

A frosted silence followed. When the handsome man gazed at Grace, he saw that her rosy cheeks had turned as pale as the moon and her lips moved without saying a word.

At last she swallowed and gained control of herself. "What are you doing here, Leo, on this cruise?"

His thick eyebrows curved and a puzzled expression grew on his face. "Traveling, like everybody else," he winked at her.

Grace said nothing.

"The truth," he confessed, "is that I reached a writer's block and hoped the vast sea would clear my mind."

"You're a writer?" She gasped. "What do you write about, Leo?"

The man squirmed in his spot. Then he sighed and stared at the stars for long moments. "Promise not to laugh?"

She nodded with an eager gaze.

"I am writing about true love," the man uttered as fast as he could. When he glanced at her again, he saw pools of water in her hazel eyes.

Grace took his hand. "Come with me, Leo, I want to show you something," she said softly and led him down the stairs, through a corridor and to her room.

They entered her cabin and Grace walked to her bed. With a swift motion, she snatched a page from the painter's block. "And I am a painter," she smiled and handed him the paper.

The man's eyes froze. He hesitantly slid his fingers on her painting as though he was touching a dream. "It cannot be..." Leo mumbled. Without a word, he took off his jacket, unbuttoned his shirt and turned around before the tall mirror. There, on his tanned back, was a tattoo: two butterflies in silhouette kissed on a tree branch under full moonlight. It was almost identical to Grace's painting. The hairs on his back rose like spears.

Grace took Leo's hand and led him to the balcony. Remembering the night she recognized Luxrider as her soul mate, she gazed into Leo's stunned eyes. "True love never dies, Luxrider," she whispered and kissed her soul mate once again.

After long moments, their lips separated but their hearts reunited. The wind caressed the two old new lovers, and the moon glowed proudly above their heads.

"I know your taste..." said the man, still puzzled.

Grace rested her head against his chest and chuckled. "My love," she said with a dreamy gaze. "Let me share with you a tale of a miraculous journey, a journey like no other."

CHAPTER 24

T he following fall, when the maple trees turned gold and red, a wild buzz sounded throughout Toronto. No swarms of bees or mosquitoes traveled in the air, only people's voices. All stood in a long line outside a glass building.

It wasn't an Apple store just before a new iPhone came out, but an art gallery. A giant orange and black banner flapped above the entrance:

"Welcome to a miraculous journey."

More than fifty paintings hung on the walls, all signed by Grace of the Monarchs. So pure and vivid they were that the mesmerized people inside turned quite emotional. There were gasps of astonishment, mixed with tears and laughter. The art went beyond mere observation; it became a profound experience, touching the depth of their souls. No one remained idle to Grace's miraculous paintings—nor to her presence.

She strolled among the astonished faces in her ancient

monarch dress. An amber braid swung behind her back, and her eyes sparkled like gems. She followed their reactions and chuckled.

"How much is this one?" A beautiful blonde lady wearing a stunning red gown and diamond necklace clasped her arm. Grace smiled and gazed at the painting. It was of a monarch butterfly gliding above the smooth surface of a lake, seeing herself for the first time. Grace read the name on the tag next to the painting—"A magical mirror"—and relived that precious moment.

"Twenty thousand!" she said to the woman without hesitation.

Her husband frowned, but the blonde's eyes blazed. "Done!" She hugged the monarch lady.

Grace had just sold her first art ever.

"Margaret..." protested the man with the blonde.

She turned to him at once. "I want this painting!"

The man turned mute and reached for his checkbook.

"Sir, fifty percent of the profit goes to the Monarch Foundation," Grace winked at the man.

He nodded with a forced smile.

"Ma'am...Ma'am..." A man in a black suit called to her. "How much is this one selling for?"

"'An orange prayer'..." smiled Grace and gazed at a flock of monarchs swarming through church windows and spinning around the people. "How much would you pay for a miracle to save your loved one?" Grace asked in a calm voice.

The man's mouth opened wide. "I guess...everything I have," he mumbled.

"Well, I ask $15,000 for this priceless miracle," she chuckled.

The man nodded with a smile and shook her hand.

"Madam Grace..." A lady with a French accent approached her from behind. She pointed with her finger at a painting and her pupils grew large. Her heart desired that one and her checkbook was ready in her hand.

"'True love is never lost'..." Grace beamed at the painting.

On the top half, two butterflies in silhouette kissed under a full moon. At the bottom, two strangers melted into each other and danced the tango.

"'True love' is not for sale, madam," said Grace kindly and hugged the disappointed lady. "It's available for free to all of us who dare to open our hearts and let the light flow."

The lady's eyes turned wet, and she kissed Grace on both cheeks.

A moment later, Grace's eyes wandered to a corner of the room. Dozens of people crowded in a line that extended to the street. In front of them, a handsome man sat behind a desk loaded with books.

"Leo Luxrider" is how the man signed his name in his

bestseller book. He handed it to an excited lady. On the front cover it was written: *Grace of the Monarchs & Her Miraculous Journey.*

At that moment, Luxrider's gray-blue eyes caught Grace's gaze, and he sent his wife a passionate butterfly kiss.

* * *

Save the Light Rider

After reading the miraculous tale of *Grace of the Monarchs*, I hope you realize how precious and amazing the monarch butterflies are. Each flap of their wings is true magic; each of their glides awakens the butterfly within us.

Now, the monarchs are in a grave danger. Their numbers are down due to habitat losses in the USA and Canada, as well as the degradation of the forests that support overwintering monarchs in Mexico.

Let's "Bring Back the Monarchs" to our life, let's have them fluttering over fields and hills and spread miracles once again.

Go to MONARCHWATCH.ORG to learn about and help save this orange jewel of nature.

Love G.H. BABAGILO

www.ingramcontent.com/pod-product-compliance
Lightning Source LLC
Chambersburg PA
CBHW020416180626
46812CB00003B/1000